Charlie saves Christmas

A Prologue to

The Chronicles of Eridul

DANIEL NICHOLS

Charlie

saves

Christmas

Cover art and illustrations by

Sheryl Soong

For my sister Sharon who could see
the beauty in the smallest things and
who was my inspiration for Charlie.

Contents

Ambush

Disaster

Fulcrum

Sacrifice

Very Bright

Just A Silly Dream

Chapter 1

Outside the tall building, the wind twisted and twirled as it hummed between the building crevices and whistled through the cracks along the window's edge as Charlotte—or Charlie, as she preferred—looked out across the sprawling city. Bright lights streamed away as far as she could see, adding their dim hue to the chilly night scene spread before her. And as the night air brushed against the window, its pulsing caress made its own kind of music that lulled young Charlie back into her bed and under the pile of covers that tried to fend off the disastrous events of the past few weeks.

And then... *scritch, scritch* at the window. And again, *scritch, scritch.*

Rubbing her weary eyes, Charlie rolled toward the wall, willing the intrusive noise to go away.

Scritch, scritch, once more.

Oh, what could it be? Her apartment was so far up, even birds rarely came to visit.

Scritch, scritch.

This time, Charlie pushed the covers back and rolled herself upright in bed, swinging her legs over the side in one motion and letting her feet come to rest on the soft... *moss*?... that grew thick at the foot of her bed.

Charlie gasped in shock, emitting an involuntary, "Wha... What?" as she rubbed her sleepy eyes to dispel the dream-like images that swam before them.

Scritch, scritch... the sound came again. This time, Charlie opened a single eye in the direction of the sound, which was down toward the nightstand that sat next to her bed. And there, on top of the narrow wooden table next to the white porcelain lamp with its pink shade perched a small bird who was pulling at the little necklace she had set there, as she did every night before going to sleep.

"Oh... oh... Sorry... sorry, there... just need... just need to borrow this!" replied the little bird, trying to pick the necklace up. And with a tremendous jump and furious flapping of wings for such a small thing, it managed to lift the necklace into the air while keeping itself aloft. It seemed as though its eye twinkled at her as it dipped and flipped about under the weight of the necklace as it rose at last and flitted away through a forest of tall trees.

"Hey, stop!" She cut herself off as her round eyes took in the sight before her and all around. Somehow, a dark and misty forest had sprung to life. Even as she took in the deep green of tall forest pines and the dark, damp browns of their thick trunks, the unmistakable scent of evergreen filled her senses. A tiny snowflake drifted down, landing on the very tip of her nose like a soft cold kiss that made her blink in surprise.

"Aunt Nonie?" Her voice was tenuous at first. Then she called again with a little more fervency, "Aunt Nonie!"

Only the faint echo of her voice replied as the last remnants of her room, save for the nightstand and bed, were swallowed up by the damp forest with its thick moss and twisting vines.

"Well, this is just a silly dream," Charlie said with a firm nod, trying to convince herself of the truth of her assertion before diving back beneath the covers. "I just need to wake up." And with that, she pulled the soft down comforter around her and closed her eyes tight, drawing her knees up to her chest in an attempt to will the strange dream to go away.

"Just wake up." The high-pitched voice was preceded by the soft padding of what could only be the tiny feet of some small animal that had jumped onto her bed. For a moment, she remained hidden beneath the pile of covers as she felt the tiny impressions of the creature move cautiously across the comforter toward her pillow.

"Just wake up," the voice repeated, and then again, "just wake up, just wake up, just waaaaaaake up." Over and over, the strange little voice repeated the phrase, saying it in different ways while prancing atop the comforter until Charlie threw the covers back in frustration—but not before the tiny creature had leapt free.

"You don't need to keep saying it!" Charlie blurted in a much louder voice than she had intended.

Charlie's abrupt movement caused the little creature to skitter behind the lamp on the small table. As Charlie looked about for the source of the noise, she spied the small sparkling eyes of a tiny furry creature. Its soft looking coat was brown with darker brown stripes running down its back from its head with a streak of white set in the middle.

"Go ahead... say it again. I dare you," harrumphed Charlie, causing the little creature to huddle further behind the lamp, though it seemed determined to communicate with her.

"Dare you... Dare you... Daaaaare you... Daaaaare yooooooooou," again, the little creature repeated the phrase over and over in different ways, growing more and more bold as it did.

Forgetting her unease, Charlie shuffled a little closer across the bed toward the nightstand but carefully kept her arms and legs firmly connected to the soft sheet-covered mattress. "You're a funny little thing, aren't you?" she asked as her unease began to subside.

"You're funny… you're funny… you're funny," the little creature yammered from behind the lamp, and Charlie could clearly see that this creature looked an awful lot like a chipmunk. With a sniff, Charlie decided to hop off the bed and onto the cool mossy ground—for just a moment, she wriggled her toes in the soft moss. "But not very bright. Apparently," she finished this thought as she straightened the long nightgown she was wearing before teasing her hair up into a messy ponytail that she secured with a light blue ribbon. If she were to be getting out of bed, she may as well be presentable.

"Veeeery bright… verrrrry bright," the little creature responded, positioning itself to keep the lamp between them.

"Well, I suppose you don't know where we are," said Charlie as she surveyed the thick forest surrounding them. This was a classic fantasy forest, drawn straight from the books her mother read to her when she was much younger. Huge thick trees reached skyward, their heavy limbs intertwining to form a dark canopy far above, but not too thick to allow the errant snowflake or too to drift down toward her. Indeed, there was a light dusting of snow on the ground around her in small patches, and every few moments, a clump of heavy snow would drop from above and splatter wetly to the ground.

As Charlie surveyed the strange landscape, she couldn't help but comment, "What a silly dream I'm having. Why, the next thing you know, the trees will be talking too."

"Oh, the trees don't talk," spoke another voice from directly behind her. It was so sudden in the silence that Charlie jumped a little as she spun around. In the act of doing so, she slipped on a smooth stone buried in the moss and abruptly fell down with a grunt.

"Hmmm... not very bright apparently," said the owner of the voice, which Charlie could now see clearly standing on its four legs behind her. The creature looked very much like a deer but was lean, with two long, spiraling horns on the top of its head. Its eyes were large with more than just a hint of intelligence.

"Welcome to Eridul, not that the name of the place will have any significance for you," the creature noted in bland tones. "Well then, go on and get up," prodded the creature. "Hopefully, you're the last of the batch today. And I must say that I'm very glad you are not connected to this large thing," in saying this the creature tapped the bed with a hooved leg. "You *are* separate from this, aren't you?" it asked inquisitively.

Charlie found herself at a loss for words, utterly shocked at the prospect of having a very real conversation with not one but three animals in this increasingly silly dream of hers.

"Well, it is much too large to move. If you have a need for your... shell, you'll just have to come back for it. We can't be sitting out here all night long after all." And with that, the creature walked gracefully around the bed, passing Charlie as it headed down what appeared to be a faint path of moss that stretched deep into the forest.

Charlie was still sitting on the ground, the cold and damp forest floor beginning to seep into her nightgown where she sat. As quickly and carefully as she could, she struggled back to her feet, brushing at her nightgown while casting looks back toward the creature that continued to move away from her. "You can't just leave me!" Again, Charlie was a bit surprised by the emotion in her voice. All of this just seemed too real for a silly old dream, all the way down to her cold bare feet and hands that were now reddened from contact with the forest floor.

"If you follow me, I won't be leaving you at all. If you decide to just sit there ... well, I suppose you will be on your own," replied the creature as it continued its slow plodding along the path into the forest without looking back. Snow continued to trickle down from the dark canopy above as Charlie frantically looked to her bed to find that it, like the rest of her room, was now fading away as if being consumed by the forest itself. In a matter of moments, only the dim light from her lamp remained, its small white bulb creating a dim sphere of light as it fought to hold the shadows at bay.

"Why are you all so mean!" grouched Charlie. But, seeing no other choice, she straightened her nightgown one last time, and after a few tenuous steps, she followed barefoot after the strange talking deer down the slick, mossy trail.

Just behind her, the little brown creature that looked very much like a chipmunk scampered down from its perch by the lamp. As she turned her gaze to it, the creature looked up and offered… "Very bright!" in reply before skittering into a clump of ferns along the path where telltale rustling hinted at its whereabouts. As Charlie continued down the path, the light from the lamp began to fade in the distance. As the shadows pressed in all around, the sounds of the wild forest seemed to grow more prominent in her ears.

Chapter 2

Joan Willard-Stewart, or Nonie, as the children called her, was exhausted as she stooped over the pile of dishes from the evening meal. The small two-bedroom apartment was freezing in the late autumn chill with leaky seals around the windows and poor air circulation in the building. There was no hope of getting maintenance to do anything with the place, as it was the last resort for struggling families, situated on the outskirts of the city near the rail line in a forgotten place known as the Eastern Flats.

The Eastern Flats had once been a busy industrial sector full of the bustle of large manufacturing yards that abutted the massive rail yard where countless tons of materials and goods flowed in and out on a daily basis. With the economic downturn over the last decade, however, the whole area had been converted to public housing, and its manufacturing facilities abandoned and boarded up, and along with them the jobs and hopes of tens of thousands of families.

But these were things of the past, long before Joan had moved in with young Cassie and Charlie. There were just a few minutes left before Joan would need to head down the hallway to the elevator to catch the train for the late cleaning shift in the city. She was happy for steady work, which was more than many could say in these lean times. Or at least, that's what she kept telling herself. Yet, she wished she could spend more time at home with Charlie, especially in light of recent events.

"Someday we'll get out of here," she whispered to no one in particular. At least Charlie's older sister Cassandra, or Cassie as they called her, had escaped, having been accepted into a private boarding school for the arts and been awarded enough financial aid to live on campus. "Well, some of us will get out of here," she whispered again with a wry smile. She fervently wished there could have been some way to keep the girls together, or at least nearby, but she couldn't afford to move closer to the school, and this was too good an opportunity for Cassie to let pass by.

But Charlie would never forgive her.

It was just she and Charlotte now, and Charlotte was entering the sixth grade. Charlie, as she preferred, was normally a sweet and active little girl, but once the semester had started and her sister left, Charlie had closed herself off. Now, all that Joan got out of her was an angry frown.

"Janet... what would you do," she muttered with a shake of her head, the memories of her sister stirring deep feelings that she didn't need on her plate right now. Joan had gladly taken the girls in after her sister Janet had disappeared in the aftermath of a terrible accident several years ago. After the authorities had declared Janet dead, Joan had been permitted to move forward with their adoption. And while at first, there had been a small amount of insurance money to support them in a little house in the suburbs, the continual downturn and lack of job availability had forced Joan to seek subsidized housing closer to public transportation that would be closer to the few available service jobs that were left in the city.

Having finished the remaining dishes, Joan dried her hands on a towel, took one last look at Charlie's closed bedroom door, and with a regretful knot in her throat, exited the small flat, locking the door behind her and leaving a note for Ms. Oldmire who lived across the hall before taking the elevators to the lobby and making the long trek back into the city.

Lingering unnoticed near the maintenance closet down an adjoining hall, the chief maintenance technician fumbled through his tool bag before withdrawing a pair of needle-nose pliers. The blue rubber on the handle was nearly worn through, looking much like he felt. Keeping this old building working was fighting a losing battle. The building owner, a despicable man named Kettle, invested next to nothing on improvements, and it was all Brian could do to keep the building up to code, especially with his maintenance team cut in half.

The work wasn't glamorous, but it was steady. The people who found themselves here were generally of two types, the unlucky and the unsavory. Differentiating between the two wasn't always as straight-forward as it should be. But here on the forty-third floor were a number of families, which was why he spent as much time as he could spare here. While he had no children of his own, surprisingly, he found the sound of kids around to be reassuring.

With a final twist to the wires, he finished his work and offered a brief prayer that this patchwork would hold for a few more weeks. Then, he dropped the pliers into his tool bag, closed and locked the door and made his way to the set of elevators just as they were closing. "Joan going back to work I'll bet," he mused aloud before clicking the down button on the console. That one was just unlucky.

Chapter 3

"I will not go a step further," yelped Charlie as she stubbed her toe for the umpteenth time on yet another hidden root in this rapidly darkening forest. Immense trees rose steeply on every side, creating a lofty canopy that entirely closed off what should have been the night sky. The air had grown increasingly chilly as they traveled, and to Charlie, there seemed to be no end in sight as her feet were now completely numb and throbbing from the cold ground.

At her pronouncement, the agile creature that Charlie had decided must be an antelope paused before turning its head back to gaze at Charlie with one round brown eye. "You are free to do as you wish, but I would caution you that soft skins like you do not fare well in these woods at night."

"So you say, but I don't see anyone besides you and me and..." Charlie paused noticing that the little bird that had stolen her necklace was settled on the top of a large and looping root and engaging in something of a tug of war with the small chipmunk.

"Hey there, give that back before you break it!" insisted Charlie in the sternest voice she could muster.

"Hey there! Hey there!" chittered the chipmunk as it tugged away at the silvery necklace.

With its beak firmly clamped onto the other end of the necklace, the little yellow bird nevertheless managed a reply, "I fffffound it... fffffirst."

"Well neither of you can have it," insisted Charlie as she quickly stepped up to the pair and snagged the locket that was dangling in the center of their tug of war.

For a moment, both little creatures held on tightly, but apparently saw the danger of doing so and let her retrieve her necklace, which Charlie immediately shoved into the pocket of her night gown.

"Now look what you've done, Mift!" twittered the little bird. "She's taken it back because you wouldn't share..."

"Veeerrry bright... verrrry bright" the little chipmunked stammered with a stern look in its eyes, crossing its forepaws in front of itself as it sat back on its haunches, clearly in disagreement with the finch.

"Yes, well, I hope you are happy," continued the little bird as it fluttered up and away from the root to a low hanging branch.

After a long stare, the larger creature turned its head back around before continuing its plodding pace through the forest without another word.

"I'm not going anywhere," pouted Charlie as she sat herself down in the middle of the path, arms and legs crossed. "I just need to wake up from this silly, silly dream," she muttered to herself, closing her eyes and attempting to force herself to wake up.

"Very well," noted the antelope, who continued to saunter away. "If you intend not to follow, I would recommend that you not leave the path. But you seem to know what you are doing... so I'm sure you have no need for further advice from me." The creature blinked once before calling to the others, "Come along you two, she doesn't need our help, and she is surely not the one we are looking for. Perhaps the others will have had better luck."

With a titter and a chitter, the finch and chipmunk looked back at the little girl one last time before alternately springing and fluttering ahead until all three were out of sight.

As the sound of their passage drifted away, a heavy hush fell over the forest, which seemed to grow even darker without the presence of the other creatures.

And there, in the darkening wood sat Charlie. Alone once again as tears welled at the corners of her eyes.

Chapter 4

"Another human child has arrived," a deep bass voice rolled from the darkness. "Shall I... collect this one as well?" After a moment, the huge form of a white tiger padded soundlessly into a space that was framed by eight massive stones. Each stone bore its own crudely shaped mark etched eons ago onto the inner facing like ancient carved graffiti. As the symbols meant nothing to him, the tiger focused on the lean figure that was perched atop a thick stone slab that had been placed at the center of the enclosure.

There at the center with a beam of light highlighting her from above perched a great blue heron who continued its work making small precise markings on a thin slab of slate with a large pointed crystal that was affixed to a claw on one taloned foot. Piled neatly on either side of the bird were two stacks of similarly thin slate slabs, presumably those that had been etched and those that, as yet, remained unused.

"Oh?" replied a voice as pointed and precise as its etching. A few moments passed with only the sound of the crystal grating against stone. At last, the heron settled the crystal taloned foot back down on the stone before taking the slate into the other foot and offering it one legged toward the massive tiger that sat framed in the opening created by the sole gap between the massive monoliths.

"Take this to the wolf pack." Again, the precise voice of the heron pierced the stillness of the space as its echo reverberated in sharp overtones from the cold stones.

"I am no errand runner," growled the tiger.

"You are what I say you are," shrieked the bird. And suddenly, with a crack of thunder, the whole of the space dimmed menacingly as the sound echoed back upon itself. The bird's eyes flashed a bright crimson for just a moment as it held the tiger's gaze in a mesmerizing stare.

Head bowed, the hulking cat padded to the edge of the central stone slab and took the slate gently into its teeth before turning and pacing back to the opening and out into the darkness.

"Everything is in motion," the bird intoned as its wings lifted to either side. "Now, we must be very, very precise." With this, the heron swiveled back to the center, lifting another slate from the stack to her right, setting this down gently before lifting the crystal taloned foot and once again making short, precise strokes.

As the tiger padded to the edge of the tree line, it set the slab down on the snow that blanketed the clearing surrounding the stone circle. He had no intention of blindly following the orders of this creature, no matter how powerful she was. His companion would arrive shortly, perhaps that would save him the trip to the wolf den. Silently, the tiger waited in the shadows of the dark forest as the thin sounds of the bird's etchings continued.

Chapter 5

"Just wake up... Jussst wake up!" Mift, the little chipmunk like creature was now hopping frantically from stone to stone in front of the slowly plodding antelope.

"I told you already that I will not put up with another spoiled, self-absorbed, human child..." Adeline the antelope noted dismissively.

"Verrrrry bright! Veeeeerrrrry bright, very bright..." Mift the chipmunk insisted.

"And why is it that you've suddenly taken an interest in human speak?" But the larger creature drew to a pause, turning around in the middle of the path and eyeing the frantic Mift with a cool gaze. "Wake up!" the smaller creature chirped one last time as if emphasizing her point. "Yes, I know that this one smells like the other. But you know as well as I that we can do nothing about that one." The staring match continued for several more moments before the antelope conceded with a sigh, "If you insist, take your brother back with you and try to bring the child along... I must go ahead, so do not be long. Meet me at the Great Stump before high time no matter what."

"Just wake up! Just wake up!" the smaller creature replied happily before bounding up the side of one of the trees and leaping at the small yellow finch who had just alighted on a nearby branch.

"Hey there... hey there... careful! You nearly ruffled my feathers, Mift," yelped the finch as he dashed back up into the air before Mift could tackle him off of the branch in her excitement.

"Just wake up! Juuuuussst wake up!" Mift responded as she bounded down the tree and back along the mossy trail, swishing ferns and clumps of snow as she went.

"Oh, Mift, what are you getting us into now..." twittered the bird before flitting off after the chipmunk without a second thought.

Adeline watched them go with a shake of her head before turning back up the path and heading still deeper into the wood. She could not shake the notion that Mift was right. The similarities between this girl and the first of these soft-skins to arrive was unmistakable, and the other had been the spark that ignited the war.

Before long, the finch and chipmunk found their way back along the trail to the spot where they had left the young human girl, but to their dismay, she was nowhere to be seen.

Salizar arrived as Mift was sniffing about the impression she had left on the ground. The small chipmunk bounced this way and that before leaping off the trail... presumably to follow a set of tracks she had found.

"Miiiiffft! Don't you go far... you know this is a dangerous part of the wood! Mift! I say, come back here before you get yourself into serious trouble," cried the bright yellow bird in a failed attempt to stop his feisty sibling. But Mift had already bounded well out of sight as she hurried in pursuit of the young girl.

"Oh bother... oh bother... and she took the key with her too... Adeline will not be pleased... not be pleased one bit." In a flurry of feathers, the finch began a dipping and diving flight in the direction his young companion had just gone, a sense of deep foreboding growing in his feather yellow chest.

Chapter 6

"Listen to me. The state is voting to cut back housing benefits again. We can't wait for that, this isn't a charity we're running, it's a business. Inform the residents. They pay, or they leave, it's that simple."

The deep voice rolled from across the heavy wooden desk in tones of near boredom. The meeting between the two men was taking place in a heavily furnished office featuring an impressive array of plaques, photos, and trophies that memorialized the accomplishments of its primary occupant, Mr. Harvey Kettle, sole proprietor of Kettle Holdings.

Sitting stiffly on the small wooden chair in front of the heavy wooden desk in his tidy but dated suit, Jonathan January, or Jinx, as he was called, busied his hands with the closed briefcase on his lap. He hated this part of the job. Lately it seemed like rent was increasing at a highly unusual pace, and he was aware of no government action as a likely cause. But arguing with Mr. Kettle was an ill-informed notion. The man was not only large and prone to violence, but he owned everything in the eastern flats of the city, including the police.

"Uh, yes, sir... will that be all, sir?" the wiry business manager replied.

"Where are my manners, Jinx... how are the kids these days... starting school by now, aren't they?" The deep voice wore a veritable sneer cloaked in feigned interest.

"Well, actually..."

"Of course they are, and you're a busy fellow. Oh... I saw your wife out shopping the other day, must be doing well over at the agency, eh, Jinx?" This time the knowing statement was punctuated by a low chuckle.

Jinx shuddered inside. Nothing escaped Kettle's notice, and the sheer amount of detailed intelligence he held on the people within the Flats was shocking if not amazing. Jinx often wondered how Kettle did it but knew precisely why he did it. For the why was one of Kettle's favorite phrases, which the large man was even now reciting.

"A man needs to keep all the details in front of him if he's to accomplish anything... Isn't that right, Jinx..."

"Yes..." was all that Jinx could manage in reply as the huge form of the man leaned over the desk which towered above Jinx's artificially shortened wooden chair.

With a laugh, the large man settled back into his cushioned seat and threw his feet onto the desk before lifting a folder stuffed with papers that he began to paw through in idle disinterest.

Sensing that this was the end of the meeting, Jinx stood quietly, clutching his briefcase, and heading toward the door. Just as he was about to exit the room, Mr. Kettle's voice rose once again from behind the folder of papers.

"You should take care that your wife doesn't spend too much. You never know when hard times will come." The statement was punctuated by a deep chuckle followed by a laugh that seemed to echo against the mahogany covered walls of the room.

Jinx hastened his steps out of the first-floor office space and into the lobby of Building fourteen. This was one of five buildings that had been designated for public housing. Each of them was laid out in an identical fashion, save for this building that housed Mr. Kettle's "low-town" office, as he referred to it. On average, the man spent one to two days per week here, handling the affairs of the five buildings and their staff while hosting various meetings and late-night gatherings for local officials and charitable institutions. Jinx had to hand it to him, Mr. Kettle knew how to play this game very well. Who would ever have thought that public housing could be so lucrative?

These musings and others filtered through Jinx's thoughts as he made his way out into the main lobby, just in time to see the familiar silhouette of one of the newer residents. *Ms. Willard-Stewart*, he thought with satisfaction as he watched her make her way across the lobby, through the revolving doors, and out into the night. *Yes... perhaps details are useful after all*, he thought with a smile.

Off the Trail

Chapter 7

The strange glowing light pulsed just beyond the moss-covered trail as if waiting for young Charlie to take notice. After a few moments, curiosity pushed the tears away, and with a final wipe of her eyes with her nightgown sleeve, Charlie pushed herself up from the ground to face the pulsing light. It looked soft, and most importantly—warm. In fact, as she continued to look at the light, she could feel a subtle warmth flowing over her like a welcome spring breeze. Involuntarily, she took a step toward it, the warning to stay on the trail fading quickly from her mind.

"More funny little things in this silly dream of mine. So... what are you then? Do you talk?" Charlie paused a moment, waiting for the light to do something, and when it did nothing, she took another step toward it. The feel of the cool, muddy ground was quite different from the soft moss. As the tip of her nightgown dipped into the mud, a dark stain began to seep up the garment along the hem, at which she frowned.

"Aunt Nonie will not like me getting this dirty, not at all." In so saying, she hiked the nightgown up and made small knots on each side at the hem to shorten the length a bit.

"There, that should do," she commented to no one in particular as she surveyed her work. As her eyes drifted back up to the light, she noted that it had moved just a bit further away from her. "So, are you tricking me, or helping me?" Charlie asked, but the pulsing light gave no response.

With a huff, Charlie took another step off the trail and then another, slowly sinking into the soft, muddy ground. It felt cool, but not as sharply cold as the tufts of snow from the path. While the mud was squishy between her toes, it seemed firm enough to walk through, as only her feet were covered. Without a second moment of hesitation, she set off after the pulsing light, which continued to keep an even space between them. For some time, she followed in silence as the light subtly shifted, first left, then right, then through a bush or over a stump as it directed their course through the gnarled roots of the dense forest.

After a bit, Charlie grew bored of the quiet and tried to strike up a conversation with the glowing orb.

"You know, I have an older sister. Yes. Her name is Cassie. She's an artist. Did you know she just went away to a fancy art school? Nonie says it's the best thing for her and that all of us have to grow up now."

Nothing but the sound of soft footfalls in the mud and Charlie's voice could be heard as she and the orb of light continued to make their way deeper into the wood. Apparently, the orb was not interested in interacting with her, but Charlie felt that this was at least making progress, and the warmth of the light felt good against the winter chill.

"My name is Charlie. Do you have a name?" Inquired Charlie. "Well, actually, it's Charlotte, but everyone calls me Charlie. You can call me Charlie too, I suppose." Charlie paused in her monologue, hoping for some sort of reply, but the orb merely moved forward in its stoic silence. "Well, I have to call you something. How about

Lux," she smiled at her own cleverness, lux being the Latin word for light, which she had learned from her sister just before Cassie had gone away to boarding school.

At the thought of Cassie, Charlie idly fingered the thin necklace in her pocket and the small star-shaped locket in the center that held the tiniest photo of her sister. It seemed like forever ago that she had given Cassie a last long hug before her sister had boarded the shuttle for school. For months, Charlie had marveled at the glossy pamphlets from the art school and dreamed along with Cassie about how wonderful a place it must be. Even when Cassie's letter of acceptance came, along with notice of her full scholarship, Charlie embraced her sister's joy. They had been the closest of companions. But now, that was all over.

The memories were so strong that Charlie barely noticed that the small orb of light had come to a stop in front of her as it merged with a tiny necklace that rested on the neck of an odd parrot-looking bird that eyed her with a cocked head.

"Oh..." she exclaimed as she too came to a stop in the slurping mud.

"Well. What have we here? I wondered how this thing would work. I send it out and it brings me back... you..." The voice came from a rather striking and powerful looking bird that sat perched on a heavy branch above her. Its feathers were mostly olive green with a brilliant orange flare along its wings, and its curved gray upper beak was both large and narrow. Bold yellow eyes watched her closely.

Charlie was only slightly less startled that this creature could talk, but could think of very little to say, and so blurted out, "I'm Charlie, who are you? And why are you in my dream?"

The alpine parrot, or kea, straightened its head slowly and fluffed its wings as it settled into a more comfortable position on the low hanging branch. It looked odd to be wearing a necklace and pendant, and Charlie couldn't help but notice the similarity between this pendant and her own, though hers was a star and this appeared to be a moon.

"Why, hello, Charlie. My name is Kraftin, and, yes, this is a very silly dream, isn't it? Perhaps you should just go back to sleep and wake up at home in your warm bed." The kea's voice was much deeper than she had expected and slightly gravelly as it spoke, and the bird's yellow eyes were so mesmerizing that Charlie found her head feeling light, and in spite of herself, she yawned and rubbed her eyes.

"I'm just in a dream. Yes. Yes, I should have stayed in my bed," Charlie replied mid-yawn.

"There, there, little girl. Settle yourself down on the ground. Really, you are indeed in your bed at home and nothing here is real at all. Close your eyes, and before you know it, everything will be back the way it was." The bird's voice drifted off in her mind as Charlie settled herself on the muddy floor of the forest, staining her nightgown more deeply with the dark coloring of the viscous mud as she did. The mud felt warm and soft, just like her mattress, and the wind sounded very much like it always did as it beat against her window on a stormy night.

In a few moments, the little girl was sound asleep, curled in a defenseless ball on the forest floor. Releasing his use of the pendant that hung around his neck, Kraftin the kea chuckled to himself as he hopped down from the branch and stiffly walked his way over to the girl, nudging her with his strong beak before nosing into her pocket and withdrawing the small necklace she had been hiding there. With a deft flip of his head, he wrapped her necklace around his own neck and with an effortless lunge, flapped himself back up to his previous perch.

"Like taking candy from a baby," he cackled. "Well, go on and bring her," he called out to the dark wood. "I certainly can't lug something that large about. Why the old hag wants a silly little girl is beyond me. A lot of useless whimpering and simpering."

As the large predatory bird continued its monologue, four dark shapes moved silently out of the darkness toward the sleeping form of Charlie. Their hardened shells glistened in the faint moonlight as they aligned themselves on either side of the girl in pairs, tilting their shells to the ground and shoveling her on to their backs. Then, stepping in unison with the girl atop, the giant tortoises moved the sleeping Charlie yet deeper into the wood.

His task complete, the large alpine parrot lifted into the air with a burst from his powerful wings and flew off expertly between the large branches of the forest—and all grew quiet once again.

Chapter 8

Joan grabbed her personal supplies as she exited the company shuttle that dropped each of the night crew at their various locations. Tonight, she had been assigned one of her favorite places, the large department store at the center of the city's retail district. The chill air gripped her as she stepped away from the warm confines of the vehicle, but it was only a few moments' walk to the rear door, where she swiped her entry key and was admitted with a buzz. Walking quickly through the back corridor to the supply cabinet, Joan grabbed the cleaning cart and began to push it to the elevator bank. As she arrived in front of the service elevators, she could see her third-floor destination clearly highlighted in bright yellow and marked *CHILDRENS.*

Stepping from the elevator, Joan surveyed her night's work. The children's section was always a mess, but it was somehow a reassuring mess. It seemed that children always managed to add something new to every little disaster they made. Adults might remove items from their racks and leave them in the changing area or laying about on another display, but aside from the odd food wrapper or spill, those sections were relatively easy to clean. Children, on the other hand, seemed to explore every square inch of space. Their hide and seek games often resulted in small display pieces being removed and sticky lollipops being dropped in ingenious places. Cleaning these areas was like its own little filthy treasure hunt.

"Well, let's see what you have for me tonight," Joan mused as she pushed her cart off the elevator and into the brightly colored spaces. "Toys to the right, babies to the left, and girls and boys straight ahead." In large empty spaces like these, Joan found it more comforting to maintain her own little dialogue, usually drowned out by the high-pitched hum of the sweeper as she made her way from section to section.

"The holidays are here already?" she mused to herself as her eyes lifted from her work to catch the newly placed ribbons, bows, and bells hanging from the ceiling over the nearest register. The decorations this year were even better than they had been in the past. Trees and ornaments and stuffed reindeer littered the area as tinsel garlands glimmered from the ceiling above in large undulating waves.

And there they were. Red winter boots with light gray changeable stocking slips and a pristine white faux fur edging highlighted by a dangling pair of tiny golden bells. "Charlie would love these," she noted as she switched the vacuum off and made her way over to the display for a closer inspection.

"Then you should get them for her."

The voice was so sudden and unexpected that Joan nearly jumped out of her skin, but with great control, she managed to contain her shock and turn slowly to the voice without hinting at her surprise.

"Oh, I'm sorry," continued the voice, which Joan could now see belonged to an elderly man with a scruffy but closely cropped gray beard and a twinkle in his eyes. "Didn't mean to frighten you like that. I'm just finishing the displays. Shopping season is upon us now." He smiled broadly at her as he bent to pick up a sack full of ornaments and supplies.

"Oh, I didn't expect anyone to be around this late," replied Joan lamely, turning back to her sweeper. "Those boots just caught my eye is all." She shrugged as she began to wind the long cord of her vacuum, frantically hoping this man wouldn't report her.

"Well, they're right cheerful they are. You should get them for... Charlie, was it? If you like them, of course," continued the strange man who seemed less threatening and mysterious with each passing moment.

"No, no... those are out of our price range I'm sure, perhaps after the season there will be a size left," she commented, lifting the vacuum back onto the cleaning cart. "Well, all finished here for now. It was very nice to meet you and a very pretty display you've made," continued Joan as she turned to move away. She was nearly done in any case, and a quick inspection told her that if she had missed anything, this would be passable work.

"Well, you have a good evening, ma'am. I'll be around the next week or so. Wouldn't want to surprise you twice." The man's smile could clearly be heard in his voice. "The name's Rupert, by the way, Kerstman. Have a good night, and, really, one meaningful gift is worth more than a sack full without." The old man winked an eye as he hefted his sack and moved off toward the toy section.

"I suppose it is," she replied without offering her own name in return. In a moment, she had gathered the supplies into the cart and returned to the elevator. One more floor, and her work for the evening would be done. Still, the image of the boots remained.

Chapter 9

"Just wake up... juuuuust wake up..." repeated the small chipmunk as she sniffed and scampered around the forest floor where Charlie had recently lain.

"Yes, yes... I know... it looks like an entire army came through here," noted the finch who was busily hopping about from branch to branch, tilting its head this way and that as it hoped to catch some small, important detail that could tell them more. "And these marks. A very large bird made these. No mistake," Salizar twittered as it hopped across the branch where the kea had perched itself. "I'm afraid this is very bad news. Very bad news indeed."

"Veeeery bright... Veeery bright," replied Mift from the ground before jumping toward the obviously trampled path that led deeper into the wood.

"Mift!" commanded the small finch. "We need help, better to return to Adeline, I say... but of course, you won't listen, will you."

"Veeery bright... very bright... very bright," replied the voice, each further away than the last.

"You don't have any idea what you're saying, do you..." twittered the finch as it took flight and dipped and dove after his friend.

"Very bright..."

"I thought not."

The pair continued their hunt, following the trail for quite some time, until they heard noises ahead, at which, both drew up quietly on a low hanging limb, looking cautiously at one another and straining to see through the thick undergrowth and the dark forest shadows.

"You found her and the necklace so soon... you are resourceful, aren't you?" A great blue heron stood solemnly in the center of a small clearing that lay just outside a circle of towering stones. A plume of gray-blue feathers arched up and away from its head, its regal neck curved regally as its sharp orange beak swished back and forth as it spoke.

Salizar knew the speaker well. Millicent was the leader of a rival faction of Woodlings. While Salizar was too young to know much more, the bit he had learned about the Great Wood was that Millicent was no one to be trifled with. After the felling of the Great Tree, the Woodlings had splintered into small factions, eventually forming two larger groups, one led by Adeline the antelope and the other by Millicent the heron. In many ways, Adeline and Millicent were similar. Having been raised as sisters, they were both highly educated in the ancient ways, but where Adeline embraced a return to the past, Millicent sought to reshape the Woodlings into a fearsome force that would not again suffer the fate that had led to the razing of the Great Tree that had been the centerpiece of their civilization. Both Adeline and Millicent sought to protect the Woodlings from a future war, which Salizar could understand, Millicent's fanaticism was simply too frightening. Over the cycles, her position had shifted from protection... to something more.

"You have what you want. Now... the star... where can I find it?" The speaker could not be seen from their hidden vantage point, but

Salizar surmised that this second voice must be the large bird that had ensnared the young human child.

"Tsk, tsk," remarked the heron. "Straight to business you outworlders always are. My guide will take you and your friend to the star, never fear. But first, perhaps you would consider one more favor for me?" The heron's voice was so precise and shrill that even Salizar felt a chill as he huddled more closely to Mift in the hollow of a branch as they continued to watch and listen.

"I've done what you've asked. I've had enough of your petty little quests. Show me this guide of yours and get some other underling to handle your dirty work." The voice was harsh, its decision final.

"Very well. But you realize... you are merely doing the bidding of someone else. I was going to offer you something that you yourself could use." The heron turned and began its stiff-legged walk back toward the opening of the stone circle.

"Let's not call me unreasonable," the voice replied cautiously. "What is it that you're talking about?"

In a sudden flurry, the brush in front of them swished violently aside as the face of a giant white tiger peered through, rows of sharpened teeth glinting dully in the night as a low growl echoed from its chest.

Only instinct saved Mift and Salizar as they fluttered and flipped to the far side of the tree where they clung like moss to the bark. Mift glowered in the direction of the tiger as Salizar shivered and tried not to move.

"What is it, Marvelous?" the hidden speaker asked with curiosity.

The tiger took a quick sniff of the air before deciding to withdraw back into the clearing. "We are being watched. We should be off," the tiger replied, its voice deep and sonorous.

"Just a moment... I'd like to hear this proposal," countered the voice again, its pronouncement punctuated by a rapid fluttering as the green-orange bird plunged to the ground in a flurry. From his hidden vantage point, Salizar could no longer see the scene but had the distinct impression of rising danger. Yet, the strange voice seemed more interested in its dealings with the heron, and soon made its way on foot into the stone grotto.

"Don't you have an errand to run, Marvelous?" the voice of the heron, Millicent, was clearly directed at the large white tiger who pawed his way back to the slate tablet that was resting in the snow where he had set it prior to his companion's arrival. Taking the thin stone carefully into its mouth once again, the large cat padded soundlessly into the wood, a deep growl echoing against the chill laughter of the heron who was now joining the other bird in the dark confines of the great stone circle.

When all was quiet again, the finch and chipmunk skipped and flitted away as quickly as possible. This was news that must reach Adeline, and swiftly. Salizar wished he could have caught a glimpse of the mysterious second bird but knew he had seen enough. Unfortunately, the human would have to take care of itself for now.

Chapter 10

Charlie awoke in darkness, her once pretty nightgown now sticky and wet. She was cold, and the ground was hard. Her hands were bound, and her eyes and mouth were covered with something that smelled old and musty. It was a nightmare. It was awful, and no matter what she did, she could not make it go away. After a moment of thrashing about, however, the constraints seemed to loosen. They felt pulpy, like vines around her hands, and with a few moments of more careful movement, she managed to get her hands free, allowing her to remove the damp and stinky covering from her face.

She sat up in total darkness, feeling smooth wet rock beneath her and not very far from her on either side as she stretched out her hands. Carefully, she tried to stand but found that the ceiling was much too low for that.

"Hello," she ventured quietly. "Hello?" her voice echoed back from the hard rock.

She had never been in a cave before but had seen a video about a cave rescue in school. This must be what that felt like. Involuntarily, she shuddered as the depth of darkness and the cold from the stone closed in around her. Yet, she knew that she needed to do something.

So far, she had taken everything as a dream from which she could wake. But what if this wasn't a dream at all? As ludicrous as that thought seemed in her own mind, Charlie knew that she must find some way to take control of her situation.

"Well, if this silly dream is not going to come to an end by itself, then I suppose I'll have to do something about it," Charlie's voice sounded firm to her own ears, but she could also sense the underlying thread of fear that gripped her.

"Why, yes, my dear, that is an excellent idea..."

At the sudden sound of this newest voice, Charlie shrieked and jumped and hit her head, crying out from the pain of that, and then started to sob as she huddled with her arms wrapped about her legs in the pitch darkness.

"Oh, my dear... please... I didn't mean to frighten you. I have been here all along... tied up next to you. I thought... I thought that you had seen me clearly," replied the voice after her sobbing began to subside. "Listen... I too am a captive... but you have found a way to get free."

"How... How can you possibly see me?" queried Charlie as she bravely choked back her sobs and shuffled her back against one of the walls furthest from the voice. "It's too dark in here."

"Oh... very silly of me. Of course, I cannot see anything, my dear, for... I am blind," replied the creature from somewhere to her left. Its voice was oddly accented, like some of the people she had met once in the international market that opened once a year in her part of the city.

"Well that doesn't make any sense," replied Charlie, now regaining more of her composure. "If you are blind and it is completely dark, then how could you possibly see me?"

"Well, my dear, you are not the quietest of creatures. You... make a lot of noise... and, well... noise helps me to see," responded the creature, who now made a few shuffling movements of its own.

It suddenly dawned on Charlie that there was only one creature she had learned about that could use sound to see... "You're a bat!" she shrieked as she shuffled herself further away from the sound of the creature's voice.

With a sigh, the creature seemed to slump, it's voice now holding a hint of sadness. "Yes... yes, everyone is frightened of the bat. I do not know why. I would never hurt you... unless of course you are a juicy piece of fruit... but I can tell that you are not, so... no. But listen. We can help each other, no? I can see, and you can help to set me free. If you do that, I can lead you out of this cave before the others return."

Struggling to control her breathing, young Charlie took several large breaths before responding, but paused just as she was about to reply as she remembered something from her science class about bats. "But I thought that bats were not blind, that they could see very well?"

"Ah... well, that is, unfortunately, a very sad story. I would be glad to tell you someday, but perhaps we could get out of this place first?" the creature responded encouragingly.

"Okay... okay. If you are tied up like you say... I suppose that you can't be one of the bad ones." This she said while slowly making her way toward the voice. "But If you try to hurt me, I will hurt you back," she threatened.

"Oh no, no... Jeremy only keeps his promises, do not worry. You will help me, I will help you, and we will become friends." His voice was so warm and gentle and yet funny sounding that Charlie couldn't help but feel more at ease.

And so, after a few more careful shuffles along the ground, Charlie reached out a tenuous hand, which touched soft, warm fur.

"Oh hooo... ha, ha... ha... sorry, that tickles," chuckled Jeremy as her hand lightly touched the top of his head between his wide ears.

"Your fur is so soft," Charlie commented offhand as her fingers worked their way down his back, between his wings, which were pinned tightly together by a cord of knotted vines that seemed to wrap him entirely.

"But of course. All bats pride ourselves in maintaining a clean and professional appearance. Just because we work the night shift, does not mean that we must be stinky and dirty." This, Jeremy said with a touch of pride in his voice.

"Oh, I'm sorry," noted Charlie as she began to tug at the vines until she found one that was not as tight as the others. She noted too that Jeremy seemed to be very large for a bat. "I guess I don't know very much about bats at all."

"No, you do not," confirmed Jeremy with a firm voice, but he then softened as he continued, "It is okay. We bats are used to these things. People often make judgements about others who look or sound or act differently than they do."

Charlie nodded in assent, and then realized that she was just nodding in the darkness behind him, and then realized even as she replied that he could probably tell that she had nodded with his special gifted abilities. "Yes, you are right. Cassie used to say the same thing to me all the time."

Charlie continued to work to free Jeremy from the tangle of vines, and after a few moments of prodding and tugging, the bonds became loose and slid to the ground.

"Ahhh," replied the bat as it shuffled away a few steps before unfurling its leathery wings in a much-needed stretch. "That feels, so good. Now, if only I had a juicy orange, this day would be perfect."

In spite of herself, Charlie laughed, something she had not done since arriving here. "Okay. Now, how do we get out of here?"

"Ah ha!" exclaimed the bat. "Now Jeremy will save you, just like you saved Jeremy. Come, we must go deeper into the cave in order to avoid the entrance you came in. That way will only result in our capture once again."

With that, the pair began a slow and careful crawl deeper into the cave, with Jeremy offering soft warnings and advice about the terrain ahead from time to time.

The Board is Set

Chapter 11

M s. Oldmire carefully read the note that had been affixed as usual to her door and smiled. She had taken a liking to Joan the moment they had met, which was only a few days after Joan and the girls had moved into the apartment across the hall.

"That woman is going to work herself to the bone. Won't be anything left for little Charlie if this keeps up," murmured Ms. Oldmire as she fiddled in her pocket for the keys to Joan's apartment and made her way over to tidy the place up and watch over things until Joan returned in the morning. Ms. Oldmire had never been able to have a family of her own, and the introduction of Joan and the girls had been like switching on the lights in a long-dark room. Their relationship had grown swiftly, and Ms. Oldmire had naturally stepped into a grandmotherly role, caring for the girls while Joan worked double shifts, helping to keep the apartment clean, and ensuring the girls got to their appointments and school activities on time.

Opening the door, Ms. Oldmire was unsurprised to find no sign of Charlie in the main living area. There were just two small bedrooms in this apartment, both down a short hallway to the left of the main carpeted room that opened directly into an eat-in kitchen with a small table. Various pieces of lovely art furnished both rooms and adorned the walls. "Yes, Cassie is truly talented. It was the right decision, Joan. Difficult, but the right decision," she commented in reference to Joan's difficult decision to allow Cassie to enroll in the boarding school. Ms. Oldmire often spoke her thoughts openly, in part because she was alone most of the time and preferred some voice to none, but here especially, she knew that more often than not, Charlie was listening from behind her closed door. These walls were thin as paper after all.

"You know, I'd have more to do if either of you made more of a mess." This she said as she picked up a few stray items that Charlie had left lying on the floor and that Joan had been unable to get to in the short time she had between jobs on these double shift days. While she worked, she allowed the sound of her simple cleaning to fill the silence. As she was straightening a scattering of school papers and mail on the kitchen table, she found a small flyer about an upcoming tryout for the girls' basketball team at the local school where Charlie attended.

"Well now, here's a sport I can get interested in," Ms. Oldmire mused. "Why, if they'd have let us play the way you can today, I would have been quite good. Did you know that we could only play on either the offense or defensive side of the court?" Ms. Oldmire prattled on in reminiscence of her own youth.

"We played sixes back then. Three forwards and three guards, each in our own half of the court. Forwards could shoot. No one could dribble more than twice before passing. As you can imagine, the scores were low. Very low."

This time, Ms. Oldmire cocked an eye toward the door of Charlie's room. Usually her stories would elicit something, a sound at least. But there was nothing at all. This was unusual. Charlie was a light sleeper and rarely fell asleep this early in the evening. Perhaps some cookies would spark something from the girl. It was normal to be sad for a time, but Ms. Oldmire was certain that it wasn't good for Charlie to mourn the loss of her sister like this. With that thought, she moved into the kitchen and began to sort out the ingredients for her famous oatmeal raisin cookies.

Chapter 12

"I was just with Mr. Kettle," the smooth, slick voice of Jinx slid around Brian's shoulders, making the hair on the back of the maintenance technician's neck straighten. Brian wasn't scared of the man, who was much smaller than he, but still, the little man found ways to get under his skin. Somehow Jinx, Kettle's bookkeeper and building manager, had tracked Brian down to his maintenance shop, which was situated in the subfloor of the building. Jinx only wandered down here when he had something specific with which to torture Brian.

"Not interested, Jinx," Brian replied as he set his tool belt and satchel down on the workbench inside the small maintenance room. An assemblage of light bulbs, wires, filters, and fuses littered the untidy space. Brian had better things to do than straighten up. He knew where everything was in any case, and anyone who came in here was either of the same mind or someone looking for trouble.

"Well you should be, Brian," replied the little man. Brian surmised that Kettle must have recently unloaded on the smaller man. Inevitably, if Jinx was going to get the brunt of Mr. Kettle's ire, he was going to be certain to pass that down the chain as far as possible.

And it was not lost on Brian that teasing and torturing the staff, and Brian specifically, was Jinx's favorite part of the job. "Rent is going up again," Jinx added as he plopped himself onto a stool, folding his hands in his lap and smiling mischievously.

Brian sighed and turned around to face the little man. "Kettle can't keep raising rent. I don't even like half the people in this tower, but the families can't handle it. I'm not even sure he's allowed to charge them extra on top of the federal subsidies in any event. You need to stand up to him, Jinx."

"Oh, like you do?" sneered Jinx in a quick retort. "His building. He can do what he likes, and besides, there will always be more renters. You still can't find an apartment this cheap this close to the train lines. People know that. They'll pay. And no matter what you think about the filth who live here... the worst of them pay... in cash." Jinx swiveled a bit on the old wooden stool and looked at it appraisingly. "It's your 'families' that continually miss their rents. Give me your tired, your poor, your huddled masses yearning to breathe free..." Jinx mocked.

The sly little man, unfortunately, made a good point. "That doesn't make it right," muttered Brian as he walked to the hook where he had hung his coat for the day. "Besides, it's nearly Christmas. You can at least wait until the beginning of the year before you steal what little joy they have left."

"Well, I wouldn't be so worried about the tenants if I were you," added Jinx casually.

Not taking the bait, Brian pulled his coat on and pushed past Jinx to the door, adding, "I worry about the building, Jinx. That's my responsibility and my job." He knew that Jinx was only now getting to the real news he had brought, and, quite frankly, Brian was too tired after a long shift to add anything more to the day.

Yet, as Brian headed through the door, he heard Jinx's overly casual voice behind him in reply. "Well, the building may not be your responsibility for much longer, not if the sale goes through."

That caught Brian's attention, causing him to pause and turn around. "What do you mean sale?" he asked with more interest than he desired to reveal. He noted that Jinx was leaning in on the stool now. Fish hooked.

"Kettle has an offer on the table. I drew it up for him, and it's the best he's gotten in years." Jinx paused only a moment before adding, "he's already told me that I'll be staying on with him, but you know how new ownership is, they usually replace the existing management team." Jinx let this linger, clearly enjoying this bit of conversation. In spite of himself, Brian couldn't help but think of the ramifications should he lose his job during the holidays. Worse, the smug look on Jinx's face intimated that he was genuinely having fun.

Brian fought to remain in control of his emotions. Jinx had worked him into emotional outbursts in the past, which had earned Brian several pay reductions and a police citation at one point. Surely, Jinx was just baiting him as usual. Brian managed to at least calm his expression as he turned around to offer a forced reply. "Well, I guess we'll just see. Mr. Kettle is never happy with any of the terms of these deals and usually kills them off after having his bit of fun."

"Oh yes, I'm sure you're right," responded Jinx with a sly smile as Brian, mind whirling, headed to the service entrance in the back of the building. As he exited, he took in a deep breath of the chill air before heading to his truck, which sat in the parking area that was illuminated by a single dim light.

Chapter 13

The bulky white tiger pawed silently through the thick forest, feeling oddly at home. Since his arrival here and the discovery that he could converse with the other creatures of this strange place, Marvelous had worked tirelessly to track down the object his former master had sent him to recover. He only wished that his thinking were as clear then as it was now. Surely this task would have been easier if it were. Why precisely he and the others had been sent was beyond his knowledge. *Forever an errand runner,* he thought ruefully. Upon their initial arrival, Marvelous had taken to learning the landscape. His trekking had uncovered a largely forested world with trees growing increasingly taller to the north and the terrain becoming rockier to the east and more verdant to the south. His path had eventually been cut off by a criss-crossing series of rivers and lakes. Clearly, this place was enormous, perhaps as large as the world from which he had come. And while it seemed a strange place, it was a place where someone like himself could gain significant advantage once he learned the rules.

Marvelous had seen strange powers at work in the circus tent where he had lived and performed, but here, the tricks seemed to be more pronounced, or perhaps magnified. In fact, these verbal thoughts were just as strange as talking to other creatures. Having concepts verbalized in his mind in the shape of human speech was almost as unsettling as everything else. But one thing he knew for certain, he was still one of the most powerful creatures here.

Still, it irked him that he was stuck running errands for that bird. She would have made a tasty snack, if not a light one, had she not found all of them almost immediately upon arrival and overcome Marvelous and his companions with a demonstration of her power. Five of them had made the crossing. The weakling bat had been taken quickly, along with two others, while he and the crafty bird Kraftin had shown enough cunning and strength to win the admiration of the powerful heron. Rather than taking them captive, she had simply put them to work while promising to share her knowledge of the object they had been sent to retrieve.

Low growls from multiple directions let him know that he had arrived at his desired location and that the wolf pack leader was close. Carefully, he placed the slate tablet on the ground, not wanting to make a second trip should he accidentally break it, and also wanting to free his jaws should he need to defend himself. In reply, he offered a deep guttural growl of his own.

"Now, now, no need to get excited, big fellow," snarled a voice from the darkness ahead of him.

"I have something for one of you called Ferris. It comes from the bird," Marvelous replied in his deep voice. Hisses surrounded him in response to his insult of Millicent the great blue heron, who Marvelous had learned, despised being referred to as a common creature.

"That will earn you no friends around here," responded the same voice, who Marvelous now took to be the wolf he sought. "You should show greater respect to those who are more powerful and wise than you," the voice continued.

"What do I care? Take the slate or do not. I am here for one purpose, and when that is done, I'll be gone again," replied the tiger as he lowered his enormous head, eyes expertly searching the brush around him for signs of movement.

The laughter that followed was as disconcerting as the response. "You cannot leave here. No matter where you may have come from, you do not hold the power to escape. Only the Master of Eridul can do that... and that one has not been seen for a very, very long time." Slowly, a wolf's pointed snout and face appeared from the darkness, its irksome smile spread in a row of sharp white teeth.

In a blink, the tiger pounced, clamping it's powerful jaws around the wolf's throat and pinning its head to the ground on top of the piece of slate before laying a heavy paw over the wolf's muzzle. Marvelous ignored the growls and howls that rose all around him, knowing that these creatures would do nothing while their leader's life was literally in his paws. Lifting his jaws away, Marvelous growled a deep reply, "I would not be so dismissive were I as weak and careless as you. Should I find that you have information about the star that I seek and are withholding it. Well... that would be a very bad day for you. Very bad indeed."

With that, Marvelous pushed back and away from the wolf, who clambered quickly back onto its feet before snarling, "Leave now while you can. Should our paths cross again, we will show no mercy, and I assure you that you stand no chance against all of us."

Marvelous showed his sharpened teeth in response and watched the wolf carefully take the slate into its own mouth before slinking back into the darkness. Indeed, these animals were all weak. Show even the slightest sign of force and they melt away without a fight. With a shake of his head, he turned slowly and padded his way back toward the stone circle, frowning as the night sky was filled with the whines and howls of the wolf pack.

Chapter 14

M ift the chipmunk and Salizar the yellow finch flitted and hopped their way back to the Great Stump as Adeline had instructed, but given the circumstances of their empty-handed return, the finch alighted silently next to Mift on a moss covered rock at the edge of the clearing.

Surrounded by an open area of grass, now covered in snow, the massive breadth of the Great Stump made it clear that this must once have been an enormous tree. Both Mift and Salizar knew well the story of how the tree had fallen, it was a tale that every Woodling was taught, though details had blurred with legend over time. Salizar was certain that he only knew half of the truth, and he was growing more certain the arrival of this child was connected.

"You two are unusually silent," noted Adeline as she ambled into the open area surrounding the Stump. "The soft skin decided not to come then?" the antelope queried.

"Wake up..." chittered Mift softly, her head turned toward the ground.

"The news is not good," embellished the finch as he fidgeted on the mossy stone.

"Oh?" inquired Adeline without further comment, making her way toward the stone upon which they were sitting.

"We followed her tracks as far as we dared," gulped the finch in response. "But... but there were so many of them. They took her to the..." the finch paused here, almost afraid of saying anything further.

"Go on." Adeline's voice was cool but calm.

"They took her to the Place of Stones. At least, that is where her tracks led." In saying this, Salizar hopped and fluttered up a few inches before settling back down nervously on the mossy rock.

"Millicent has her then, and that means she was indeed carrying the key," sighed Adeline who turned and strode back toward the Stump. "Worse... if the child carried the key... it is possible that she is also... " Here, Adeline censured herself, keeping whatever thought she was about to voice hidden within. Instead, she shook her head slowly and concluded, "There are so few of us these days. I'm afraid that Millicent has gathered too many of the Woodlings to herself." Turning her large eyes back toward the small pair, she paused a moment before adding, "I'll need you to find Old Pete." Adeline watched the pair closely as if to gauge their response.

"Heeey there... hey there. Hey there!" chittered Mift as she began to hop up and down and scurry about on the mossy stone.

"All will be well," stated Adeline in a firm tone, now turning around fully to face the pair of them. "I don't like it any more than you, but I must gather what's left of the Woodlings who are willing to stand against Millicent. I had hoped it would not come to this, but it seems that Millicent is indeed moving her insane plan forward. I need you to find Old Pete and convince him to help us."

"But... but..." chirped Salizar.

"I'll have no excuses, Salizar. You did not bring the girl or the necklace. This is now our only option." Adeline added a long hard stare at the end, which Salizer took rightly to mean that her opinion was firm and that this was not a request.

"Hey there..." replied the chipmunk glumly before nodding to the finch, hopping off the stone, and disappearing back into the forest.

"Mift and he do not get along," pleaded Salizar. "You know he tried to eat Mift the last time." This final sentence was chirped as Salizar lifted from the stone in a hop and began to flitter into the air, anxious to follow after the impetuous Mift.

"Trust me... I know all too well. But Pete can help. I hope." This last, Adeline spoke into the quiet clearing, then turned and with a tenuous step, leapt to the top of the Great Stump. "Now to call the woodlings," she muttered as she cast a look out to the darkening tree line.

Chapter 15

"So, this deal. What do you have in mind?" Kraftin asked after settling himself to the left of the opening between the great monoliths whose ancient shapes secured the sacred center. Each towering sentinel featured a deeply grooved carving, some familiar, some entirely foreign to him. The carved mark on the stone to his back looked very much like a snake, but he paid no mind to the silly scribblings of this strange world.

"Patience, patience," replied the heron demurely, its long legs carrying it to the far side of the stone grotto in a circuitous route. As she passed each massive stone, Millicent took a moment to take in the shape before moving to the next. The movement struck Kraftin as threatening, though it was nothing more than a quick gaze meant to appear incidental. "You are an outworlder. There have been more of you in recent cycles. But there is something... different about you and your friends," she noted while appearing to study another odd mark, this one looked like a crashing wave.

Kraftin watched the taller creature with a cold eye. He could be patient, but he also felt that this one was just trying to play him for a fool. "As I told you already, we were sent here to retrieve something."

The kea's voice echoed slightly from the cold stones that towered all around and above. He estimated that they must be nearly six meters each, not nearly as tall as the circus tents, but massive and impressive, nevertheless.

"Yes, yes ... the Celestial Star, you say." Again, the heron replied in her smooth and calm voice. "Others have been looking for the same thing... many come and go and never find it. Perhaps it is just some silly tale you share with one another... a false treasure that you seek." The heron passed yet another stone, this one featuring what appeared to be a powerful stag in mid leap.

"But YOU say you know how to find it... if not, we are wasting our time here." In spite of himself, Kraftin ruffled his feathers and stood taller, cocking his head to one side as he eyed her like prey. This bird had gained his respect instantly upon his arrival by somehow silencing and stunning all five of the small group that had made the crossing. Only he and Marvelous had recovered quickly enough to gain their feet and protect themselves, which had earned them a chill laugh and a handful of chores.

The heron's raspy voice scraped the air like brittle metal on glass, bringing him out of his memories as it reverberated in frail overtones throughout the tomb-like resonance of the stone circled enclosure. "Do you have any idea what the star you seek is?" This time the heron spoke in a whisper, turning her head at last to look toward the muscular kea. "How silly of me, of course you do, since you wear its moon twin." The heron had come to rest in front of yet another of the large encircling stones. After gaining Kraftin's attention, she slowly turned her gaze to the stone and up to the markings etched onto its solid face.

Following her gaze, Kraftin could see what appeared to be an etching of a star surrounded by concentric circles with a large moon in orbit around it. It was then that he noticed the orb around his neck glowing softly. A tingling sensation suddenly filled him as it had before when he'd lured the child to his trap. Yet, this time, he could feel the slight surge of power through his wings and down into his talons. For a moment, he felt stronger, larger, and then the orb faded, and with it the strange sensation.

"Yes. You see now, don't you," continued the heron. "You come to us seeking something from our realm, but you bring with you something of near equal power. Something that we have been seeking for… many cycles. Twelve such keys were made in the days of old, any two of which could be used together… to unlock a passage to the outworlds to which they were bound. But in the aftermath of the first Outworlder War, two were lost, sealing off our path to the most important outworld of all: Maridil… your home. I had wondered what shape they might take… silly that they should be as obvious as this… a star and moon indeed…" The heron had grown larger as she spoke, and a thick vapor began to pour from the base of the large surrounding monoliths.

With a flurry, the kea launched himself into the air, gaining altitude rapidly and swooping around the enclosure, seeking the right angle at which to strike. Having been trained to perform stunts in the interior of a circus tent gave him a decided advantage in the confined space of the enclosure.

"Ah… so you do have some spirit, don't you," continued Millicent as her form settled back into her original size, and the darkness dissipated. "I will not take it from you. On the contrary, I have a proposition for you. You see, I believe your master sent you here to retrieve something that was already in your own world. And now it seems that both keys have returned of their own accord."

Finding no other place to alight, Kraftin swooped back to his original position near the opening of the stone structure and folded his wings while keeping a sharp eye on the taller bird. "Do not play me for a fool… either of us. We may not be of this world, but we are not easy prey like your other outworlders may have been." It was only then that his keen eyes saw the hundreds of tiny pieces of bone that littered the ground around the large stone slab and within the cracks that ran across its surface. The heron's cold crackling laughter interrupted his thoughts as this realization struck him.

"Come now. Let us be allies. Together, with your moon and my star, we can rewrite all of reality. In this world… in any world." With that, the heron flapped to the top of the flat stone altar that lay in the center of the circle and beckoned with a wing for him to do the same.

After a moment's pause, Kraftin hopped atop the stone table and cautiously approached the other. "An alliance then. Tell me what you need me to do," Kraftin replied as he watched her lift her crystal-taloned claw to another thin piece of slate.

Chapter 16

"This is unusual," Mr. Kettle noted as he settled himself into a plush chair in the small conference room on the first floor of building fourteen. "We could just as easily have met in my corporate suite downtown," he continued as he leaned back in the chair. "I am reviewing your proposal, and as I told your lawyers, I'll let you know if I'm interested in selling." This time he leaned in and settled his arms on the table, staring intently at the man who sat opposite him.

"Oh, that's fine. I'm just old fashioned, you might say," replied the businessman who was behind the recent generous offer for Kettle's buildings.

The offer was so generous, in fact, that it had given Kettle pause. He had been trying to sell these buildings for years at a fraction of the price this man, or the company behind, him was willing to pay. "Kerstman, is it? I haven't heard of you or your company, and I've been in real estate in this city for decades." Kettle would normally have gladly taken the offer, but since he already had the upper hand, he saw no reason not to push for more. What could this man possibly want with a run-down tenant building like this?

"Oh, I am merely the representative of a larger multi-national. We have holdings in most of the large cities. It's a simple business really, we are creating a globally available community of affordable housing. Our tenants assist in the upkeep and safety of our facilities in exchange for lower rents. I have been looking at the buildings across this city, and your properties here seem to fit our interests quite well," Kerstman replied in his jovial voice.

Kettle did not like this man at all, acting like a big fish in his city. He certainly didn't need a competitor in the subsidized housing market. This building was one of five that were veritable cash cows for him, even if they were long overdue for significant and costly improvements. For several moments, Kettle thumbed his chin while studying the older man. The man seemed to be rather unremarkable in most every way. He neither dressed well nor poorly. He sat straight but relaxed, his handshake had been firm, but his mannerisms were one of an old man past his prime. He walked with a slight limp and spoke with a hint of a lisp. He was the perfect mark.

"Well, I'm sure you'll find that we run a tight ship around here, Rupert," commented Kettle in the midst of this introspection. He had learned a few tricks in his years of negotiating, and loved the game almost as much as he loved winning it. All he really needed to do was to discover what it would take to make this man uncomfortable. "A strange name you have there, not very common, must have given you a rough time in middle school with that, eh?" Kettle sneered at the man as he leaned back into his chair. He loved to push people's buttons, though his sneer lessened as he noted that Mr. Kerstman was already standing.

"Well, it's been wonderful to meet you. I have the keys from your agent and permissions from your lawyers to do a foot inspection. I've already seen the floor plans, so don't worry about feeling as though you need to show me around. No one ever notices an old man, do they." Kerstman's smile broadened as he picked up his briefcase and turned toward the door.

Rushing to his feet, and nearly overturning his chair in the process, Mr. Kettle offered a hand, too late, as Kerstman had already turned away. Not wanting to end the conversation just yet, Kettle made his way quickly around the large central conference table to intercept the old man at the door. Reaching him just in time, he placed a thick hand on Kerstman's shoulder, "Well, that's just fine. Feel free to have a look. Just take care not to disturb the residents. And be careful on some of the floors. We try to keep things orderly, but we can't keep out all of the riff raff." He gave the man's shoulder a squeeze, finding him oddly solid for such an old looking fellow.

Kerstman looked down at Kettle's hand on his shoulder long enough for Kettle to smile and give him one last squeeze before taking it away. "Yes. People can be unpredictable," the older man noted as he prepared to step into the hallway leading to the lobby and the bank of elevators. Both men paused as they made to leave the conference room, however, as a young man in coveralls strode swiftly by before exiting the building without a backward glance. The first man was followed almost immediately by a second individual with thin slick hair whose face bore a wicked grin that slid swiftly away as he caught sight of Mr. Kettle standing in the frame of the door with Kerstman.

"Ah, there's Jinx now. If you want to go over the papers again, that's my bookkeeper." Hearing his name called, Jinx nodded before slipping into an open office door along the same hallway, as if this were what he had intended all along. In the brief moment that Kettle had taken his eyes off of the old man, Mr. Kerstman had somehow managed to reach the bank of elevators down the hall in the opposite direction and was smiling back as the doors slid closed with a dull thunk. Indeed, Kettle was liking this man less and less all the time.

Gone Missing

Chapter 17

"You know it helps very much if you talk a little. Your voice helps me to see in the darkness." Jeremy's statement startled Charlie out of her momentary thoughts of home. It seemed like days had passed since Charlie had actually seen light, but her mind's eye had been quite active, replaying memory after memory of younger happier days with her sister.

"Oh, okay... umm, what would you like me to talk about?" Charlie replied from behind Jeremy as she felt her way along the cave floor, trying not to bump into the rocks and cave fixtures that littered the place. Jeremy had kept up a slow stream of conversation to inform her of how best to maneuver herself to avoid trouble as they made their way deeper into the cave. For a long while, they seemed to be going down and down, but now, the path felt as though it were moving back up again.

"Well, that should be easy. Why don't you tell me about you? I know nothing," his voice echoed back as he continued to make slow and steady progress forward. "How about we start with your name, for I do not even know that much about you."

Charlie blushed, though no one would see it in the dark, perhaps not even Jeremy, as she realized that while he had introduced himself, she had not responded in kind. "Charlie. My name is Charlie. Well, actually, it is Charlotte, but everyone calls me Charlie."

"There! One fact about Charlotte," the bat laughed, his voice echoing deep within the cave. "If you do not mind, I love the name Charlotte and would call you by your full name, but only if you permit." The large fruit bat had paused in front of her, his voice growing louder, as presumably he had just turned around to face her.

"I guess that's okay," Charlie responded timidly. He was such a friendly creature she couldn't help but smile at his enthusiasm for the smallest things.

"Excellent. Now, another fact about Charlotte. Tell me more, for your voice lights the path before us."

She could hear the smile in his tone and chuckled in response. "Well, I'm not very interesting. My sister, she's much more interesting than me."

"Ah ha! Two facts! Two facts about Charlotte. Charlotte has a sister. Does this sister have two names like you?"

"Actually, yes, she does," Charlie responded, as she started to warm to the conversation. "I call her Cassie, but her full name is Cassandra." And in saying her name, a deep sadness welled inside of her, choking her throat momentarily. "I miss her so much," she whispered.

"Oh... my dear, I am so sorry. Is your sister no longer alive?" Jeremy had paused his movement again, his voice softening in his response.

"Oh no, no. She just had to move away to a new school," Charlie replied sullenly.

"I see. Is this school you speak of some terrible place where they torture Cassandra? Perhaps it is dark like this cave with no fruit. Not to ever see a beautiful fruit again would be terrible indeed." Charlie could hear Jeremy drawing back toward her as he responded, his voice soft and empathetic.

"No, it's not like that. She's actually in a really nice place. You see, Cassie is a really good artist, so she went to a special school where she can become even better." She didn't know why but explaining it like this didn't make it seem so bad.

"Well then, why is Charlotte so sad? If your sister is not in danger and she has fruit, what could be so bad?" Jeremy seemed to relax again and must have turned around as she could sense him starting to move forward.

"Well, I don't get to see her. I mean, she'll be home in a few weeks for the holiday break, but I didn't get to go with her." Again, Charlie's own response seemed to lessen how badly she felt about the whole situation.

"Ah, you miss her. This I understand. But it is good that you will be seeing her again, and soon, no?" Jeremy spoke in reassuring tones as the pair continued to move through the darkness of the cave.

"Yes, I guess. I guess I just miss having her around. I don't have anyone to talk to anymore except for my Aunt, and she's just a grownup." Charlie felt like she was realizing this for the first time, and even as she spoke, a weight seemed to lift away.

"Well, now you have Jeremy to talk to. And your sister will be home soon, and Jeremy will help you find your way back, and everything will be wonderful again!" Jeremy's voice boomed through the cave, his jovial spirit returning. "So, tell me. This place where you are from. What kind of fruit do they have?"

"Well, we have all the normal fruits like apples and bananas," Charlie noted, smiling again.

"Ha! That sounds wonderful! Perhaps Jeremy will be able to visit this place and try your apples and bananas."

The pair continued to make their way through the cave, their conversation echoing softly against the cave walls as they traveled, now more easily through the darkness.

Chapter 18

"He'll be near the caves, Mift. And you don't have to go if you don't want to." Salizar had finally caught up to the scampering form of Mift, who was making excellent time in her journey along the forest floor. While it had taken most of the day, they were getting close to the last place anyone had seen Old Pete. In many respects, Old Pete was a bit of a legend among the Woodlings, not only due to his advanced age, but likely also because of his reclusive nature. It was believed that he inhabited a region of rocky caves that sat to the east of the Great Stump, creating a triangle between the Stump to the north and the Place of Stones to the south. While many stories and rumors surrounded the enigmatic bird, Old Pete, who was a kakapo—or large, flightless, parrot-like bird—was someone with whom both Salizar and Mift had personal experience.

"Heeeeyy there..." chittered the chipmunk as she hopped on top of an old log, pausing to sniff at the air.

"I'm sure he didn't mean to almost eat you," continued the finch as he alighted on the log next to the chipmunk. "He's just a little loopy in the head, that's all."

"Veeeery bright... very bright," responded the chipmunk as she dashed back into the underbrush.

With a shake of his head, the finch leaped back into the air, fluttering after the chipmunk, and was almost knocked completely out of the air by a blast of water and foam that shot past him in mid-flight. "Look out, Mift! Incoming!" chirped Salizar as he swooped and darted expertly to avoid a second streaming blast of water.

"Wahll what do we have 'ere?" a familiar voice croaked, the sound of the voice clearly ringing from the source of the water barrage.

Wheeling back around and through a tangle of brush, the small finch popped out into a stony clearing at the front of what looked like the mouth of a large cave. And there, standing before him was the large parrot-like form of Old Pete, who held some sort of brush in one hand as he scrubbed furiously at the inside of his beak, before dashing his head into a shallow pool of water before spurting it out of its mouth in a stream that this time, thankfully, was not aimed at Salizar.

Mift, meanwhile, had scurried up on top of a short boulder that set her nearly eye level with the large and wizened figure of Old Pete.

"Hey there... hey there..." Mift tittered as she settled in a spot where the old warrior could see her, eyeing the large bird with a glare.

Old Pete was one of the last of his kind, or perhaps the only one of his kind. Unlike other bird-like creatures in the Woodling community, he could not fly at all, though his wide taloned feet allowed him to easily climb trees, and his stumpy wings permitted him to parachute down from great heights. He was nevertheless a handsome bird with bright green plumage and a strong, curving beak. Pete was also exceedingly strong, if not a little on the dim side, which was likely a result of his advanced age or perhaps having taken one too many rocks to the head during the War with Maridil, of which he was the only known living survivor. In fact, no one knew how old he was, as it seemed he'd been around before anyone else.

"Hey there yourself, little fellow," the ancient kakapo responded, tossing the stick it had been using to the side before letting out a strange barking bellow, which was apparently it's laugh. "Say, didn't I eat a critter just like you not too many cycles ago?" The large green bird tilted its owl-like face to the side, eyeing Mift who grandly stood her ground.

"Now, now, Great Pete, we, we don't mean you any harm. We've been sent by Adeline with terrible news," interrupted Salizar, who was ready to be off that topic as quickly as possible. The much smaller bird zipped past Pete in an attempt to redirect his gaze before alighting on a perch opposite that of his companion, Mift.

"Terrible news, you say. How delightful," croaked the large bird, who settled down on the ground as if awaiting a grand tale. "I haven't heard news in such a long time, good, bad, terrible, or otherwise." His eyes seemed to smile at the diminutive finch, but Salizar was not about to let his guard down.

"More outworlders have arrived," Salizar began, but the large kakapo interrupted him immediately with a loud barking bellow.

"Bah! outworlders, inworlders, woodlings, stonelings, wild-lings… next you know, that Adeline will be trying to get me to raise the Stone Army again. What a lot of rubbish. If that's all you have, perhaps I will eat this friend of yours," and with that, the large bird hopped back to his feet and waddled toward Mift, who skittered quickly out of sight.

"I know nothing of that, but I did meet one of them, a young female soft skin who had a locket with her. And… and Millicent has her now." Salizar had already swooped up into the air and was flittering about in agitation with the news, once again trying to divert the larger bird's attention away from Mift.

"Well now. A soft skin. See now that is interesting." The large bird nodded before retreating to his prior seat before continuing. "Please, tell me more."

As he was saying this, strange echoing sounds began to emanate from the cave mouth behind him, drawing the attention of all three of them.

Chapter 19

His hand throbbed as he sat outside in the chill night air. Brian knew it was idiotic to let Jinx get under his skin like that, and even more idiotic to try to take it out on a cold metal light pole. How people like that and people like Kettle managed to get ahead, he just couldn't understand. Brutal, nasty people always came out on top. He was in the middle of this dismal line of thought when a pair of worn looking shoes came to a stop right in front of his downcast gaze.

"I hope you don't mind," noted a voice he recognized as Joan from the forty-third floor, "I'm sorry, perhaps this is a bad time, I'll just file the ticket tomorrow," the voice continued. And then the shoes were walking away.

Joan had walked several steps past the maintenance manager by the time Brian's mind pulled itself from his funk. "No, no, I'm sorry. It's alright, just… I was just preoccupied is all." Slowly, Brian pulled himself to his feet, shoving his reddened hand into a coat pocket. "What can I do for you, Ms. Willard… err, Stewart?" he added lamely.

Joan turned around and smiled up at him. He was, after all, a rather tall man, and she was petit. To Brian, that smile was like a warm blanket, and he caught himself in the middle of an oddly lopsided grin.

"I'm so sorry to bother you, it's just the vents again. We just aren't getting good air circulation, and I thought maybe you could send someone up?" Joan smiled up at him again, and for some reason, all thought of his throbbing hand melted away.

"Oh, yes, sure. You're in apartment number?" Brian stammered. He knew well what apartment she lived in, but even in this slightly addled state he understood that her knowing that he knew... might be disconcerting.

"Apartment forty-three twelve," Joan responded quickly. "I'll be out most of the day and evening tomorrow and the next day, so just let yourself in. Ms. Oldmire and Charlie should be in there and can point you to what I'm talking about." Again, the bright smile, this time highlighted by a sprinkling of snowflakes that had begun to fall from the dark night sky.

Brian wondered how someone like Joan could even find a way to smile. Even if he lost his job, he was in a better situation than her with her two girls and two or three jobs. Brian had a favorite coffee mug and an idea of a dog he might get someday, but outside of that, he had no one else relying on him. "Oh yes, forty-three twelve, can't forget that, just one two three four in a different order," he added and immediately regretted himself. Why on earth he got so flustered around her, he had no idea. "Oh, and, Joan," he continued hesitantly.

"Yes?" she asked, again, blinking this time and laughing lightly as a snowflake landed lightly on an eyelash.

Brian sighed. He just couldn't tell her about the possibility of rent going up. Let her be happy at least another day or two. "I'm sorry, ma'am, that your airflow isn't working properly. I'll look into it myself." Well, he supposed that was better than nothing.

"Oh, I understand that you're busy, and it's a very large building. You don't have to do it yourself... but thank you all the same. Good night, Brian," she said before turning and heading back inside the building.

"Yeah, um, good night, Ms...." Brian trailed off. How did one handle these hyphenated names anyway?

Chapter 20

Having busied herself with everything she could think of, and there only being a few minutes remaining until Joan returned, Ms. Oldmire decided to peek in on the unusually quiet Charlie. Slowly turning the doorknob to the bedroom, she opened the door soundlessly, the smile growing on her face as there was nothing sweeter in this world than the cherubic face of a sleeping child. The room was dark within, but Ms. Oldmire could make out the typical trappings of a young girl's room. There were drawings from her sister on the wall, a few stuffed animals and clothes strewn about. Ms. Oldmire tsked softly at this. Charlie was such a mess, a sweet little mess but a mess all the same. Her eyes cast to the rumpled covers on the bed and then narrowed as she noticed that the covers had been thrown back, but Charlie was nowhere to be seen.

Opening the door a bit wider, Ms. Oldmire stepped a foot into the dark room and craned her neck to see if perhaps Charlie was bundled into the bottom corner of the bed, or perhaps had just slipped down onto the floor. A surge of alarm and concern hit her chest when further inspection revealed no little Charlie sized shapes to be found anywhere in the room.

"Charlie?" Ms. Oldmire whispered at first, but then stepped fully into the room and walked up to the bed. "Charlie? It's Goldie here." Goldie was the name Charlie had given her on account of the collection of gold necklaces that the old woman allowed Charlie to model from time to time.

Her voice raised to normal speaking tones now, Goldie reached for the light and switched it on. "Charlie? Come, dear, this little game isn't funny. Your aunt will be home soon, and you should be in bed." Still no reply. At this point, Goldie turned over the covers, stooped to peer under the bed, and looked in the closet, pushing the hanging clothing from one side to the other.

Yet, there was no sign of Charlie anywhere. "For goodness sake, where did you go, girl?" Her heart was beating much faster now, thoughts swirling through her mind about how she would be blamed for all of this and of what possibly might have happened to the little girl.

"Did you run out before I arrived? I came at my normal time. Come on, dear. Charlie? Charlie!" Ms. Oldmire began to move through the rest of the apartment, not that there was much to the place. She checked Joan's room and the laundry room, as well as all of the closets and the lone bathroom, but there was simply no sign of young Charlie.

As panic was setting in, the door to the apartment opened, and in walked Joan, who stopped immediately as she saw the ashen look on Ms. Oldmire's face.

"Charlie's missing. I… I don't know where she is."

Chapter 21

Word travels quickly in most circumstances, and bad news travels the most quickly of all. By morning, the forty-third floor was abuzz with whispers about a missing girl, and by noon, it was the talk of all of Building fourteen. For Jinx January, it must have seemed like Christmas morning itself had arrived early with the most wonderful gifts.

"How salacious! You don't say. A girl of eleven missing on the forty-third? How dreadful." He made a marvelous show of concern on his face as the tenth tenant shared what little detail they had heard. On the whole, the story had remained relatively the same, but given the 'encouragement' Jinx had offered in the form of a month's free rent for anyone willing to come forward with 'evidence' of the mother's neglect, the rumors were far more salacious than what Ms. Filmore had expected to encounter upon arriving that morning. If she could count on anything, it was the sinister state of the human condition. Offer a little reward, and people would sell their own mother. Ms. Filmore stifled a frown as she watched Jinx's smile grow with the growing parade of 'witness' testimony.

One said it was the old woman across the hall who stole the child away from her negligent mother. Another said that the child merely ran off to find her sister who had been thrown out of the apartment. Still another claimed that the girl had been so badly neglected that she had died, and her body had been found in the laundry chute. Jinx seemed to bask in the inventiveness as each new voice built a case against the woman whose child had gone missing. For her part, Ms. Filmore listened quietly and jotted notes as she watched and observed. At this rate, Ms. Filmore would not have been surprised to find the local news station parked outside, though she was also amazed at how rapidly the situation had escalated. The girl had only been missing since the night before.

"Well, as you can hear for yourself, Ms. Filmore, this is certainly something that child protective services should look into. I don't have any idea what could have happened to the young girl, but we at Kettle Holdings take child safety very seriously, which is why I called you over here personally." Jinx smiled broadly, a sinister caricature of the clean-cut service officer that sat before him in her prim dark suit, briefcase in hand.

"I suppose that it cannot hurt to take me to the room. I assume that the mother is there now?" Ms. Filmore had seen and heard everything. Literally. Cases like this, fortunately, usually turned out to be nothing more than a child running and hiding and then returning when they were hungry again. Though, much worse could be at play here, and that was what she was trained to handle. Still, she could not shake the idea that something more sinister was at play with the timing of these circumstances.

"Oh, I believe so. She is certainly making a good show of being frightened. Did you know that this isn't the girls' real mother? No, no, this is her adoptive aunt. The poor young girl lost her mother some years ago and has been in the care of her aunt since arriving here.

Sadly, the poor woman can barely make ends meet and is always away working, leaving the young child alone most of the evening and night when school is out. Or at least, that is what I hear." Jinx smiled again and then stood. "If you are ready, you can follow me."

Ms. Filmore was a good judge of character, and this character she did not like, but no matter who or what he was, he was not likely at fault here, just another leech feeding off of the pain of others. But this she expertly kept to herself as she stood as well and nodded. "Yes, please, I think I will interview the mother now, and the care-taker who lives across the hall? Ms. Phyllis Oldmire, is it?"

"Oh yes, Ms. Oldmire. She has been a resident for many years. Keeps to herself mostly. I wouldn't have thought she could do anything to harm anyone, but, who knows," Jinx chuckled lightly. "Stranger things happen, and these days you just never know." This last he said as he walked out the door, leading Ms. Filmore to the bank of elevators and clicking the button for the forty-third floor.

Chapter 22

The small, silver, star-shaped locket lay in the center of the great stone altar, that itself sat at the heart of the grotto with its towering stone monoliths encircling like ancient wardens. Lifting the crystal that was affixed to one of her talons, Millicent touched it to the tiny clasp before closing her eyes and taking in a slow deep breath. All around her, darkness began to flow in thick tendrils from the base of the stones whose odd carvings glimmered with an evil light.

Kraftin the kea watched with keen interest. At first the effect appeared similar to the fog machines that his master would use in one of the Circus shows. But these tendrils clung together and moved more like snakes, as though they had a mind of their own. Each large monolith produced a unique number of these foggy extensions, which swirled together as they converged upon the heron and the stone upon which she stood. Kraftin had half a mind to touch one of them but something in the back of that mind was warning him against doing so.

Millicent cackled like a creature gone mad and with a sudden downward motion, stabbed the locket, which sprang open with an audible click. As the locket opened, it appeared to generate a force of its own, as all of the dark tendrils began to pour themselves into both halves of the open star shape until the locket was vibrating and glowing with a faint blueish hue, not unlike that of the moon shaped orb hanging around Kraftin's neck.

With a slowly exhaled breath, the heron opened her eyes and turned to the Kea while still pinning the locket to the stone with the tip of the crystal. "Now. Take it and place it around your neck. Do it quickly and clear your mind of anything but your desire for the Celestial Star."

Kraftin approached carefully, picking up the encircling chain first and marveling at the trick of shadow and light he saw before him. His own master performed such feats with regularity, but usually there was some machine involved. Here, there seemed to be nothing creating all of this. Still, if this was all he needed to do in order to gain access to his prize, then so be it. He would play her silly little game.

With a swift motion, the kea tossed the necklace and glowing locket into the air, snagged it in his curved beak, and flipped it one last time around his head, letting the locket fall around his neck once again. As he did so, everything around him exploded in pain, color, light, and sound. It was like nothing he had ever experienced in this world or any other. He could hear his own shrill cry echoing all around him, fusing with the cackling laughter of the maniacal heron. It was all he could do to pump his powerful wings, and in a few moments, he could sense that he was aloft, twirling and spinning in an aerial dance, the likes of which he had never dared dream to perform.

Below him, the heron looked on, her face a mask of glee as the light of the locket spread first across the kea's chest and then to the tips of his wings until his whole feathered body was framed in blue-tinted light. Then, with a surge of power, Kraftin launched upward, and like a flaming, shimmering phoenix, began twirling about, each swooping dive scorching a hissing mark of light through the air in the shape of one of the ancient symbols that was etched into the surrounding monoliths.

Quickly, the heron began to scratch what it saw on the flat slate tablet at its feet. "At last! The Ancient Powers will awaken and I… Millicent the Great, will take control of this realm and all others as the prophecy has foretold!" Helplessly Kraftin twirled as the Millicent's maniacal laughter bore into his skull.

Battle Cry

Chapter 23

Joan leaned against the sink feeling sick. "I believe you, Goldie, I believe you. Charlie has been distant since her sister left." Joan's voice cracked with emotion. What would her sister think of this? "She must have... must have waited for me to leave and snuck out just after I closed the door. It's just... why would she take nothing with her?" Joan's mind wasn't working well. Each thought seemed to appear as if through a soupy fog, quick to drift away. Only the firm feel of the cool stainless-steel sink felt substantial.

Phyllis 'Goldie' Oldmire stood quietly at the edge of the kitchen, where the linoleum floor tiles were joined to the worn carpet of the living room by a thin strip of dented metal. Joan could feel her anticipation as the shock of the news that Goldie had delivered rolled through her mind. "I came over when I normally do. I would never believe that she might run off like that." Ms. Oldmire's voice sounded frail and began to waver with emotion as she continued. "I can look for her, Joan. This is my fault—I should have come over sooner." Ms. Oldmire had a hand on the door latch when Joan finally broke the lengthening silence.

"No, no, I can do that. It's me she's angry with, and I'm used to the walking. She could have gone anywhere, but without her coat, hopefully she is smart enough not to go outside." She pushed herself back from the sink and pulled her hair back, tying it in a loose ponytail behind her head. "Can you stay here? I hate to ask that of you, but if she comes back while I'm out, it would be good to have someone here." Joan was already making her way to the door. She just needed to find her daughter quickly and get this behind them both. Even as she was thinking this, a flash of anger swirled within the sphere of her rising fear. Of all the mean tricks to play, running off was one she never thought Charlie would do.

"Of course, of course I'll stay. You go and look. I'll be here." Joan took note of how Phyllis had managed to steady her voice as she passed by. There was no hiding her red-rimmed eyes and exhaustion after coming off a nearly forty-eight-hour shift. When Phyllis spoke again her voice was calm and filled with concern, "We'll find her, Joan, don't worry, I've seen these things before. We'll find her, or Charlie will return when she's cold or hungry." Ms. Oldmire nodded in an attempt to reassure them both of the truth of her own words.

"I know. I'll be back soon." With that, Joan left the room and started to make her way first through the forty-third floor. As it was still late, she called softly every once in a while for Charlie and spoke quietly with the few people she met in the hallway. Everyone was kind but assured her that they had seen no little girl recently, but that they would keep their eyes open.

Joan felt sick as she continued her search through the night. Each person she told, each knowing look was another person that knew of her plight. She understood all too well that each conversation was like setting a spark in a dry forest. The resulting inferno may well have monstrous consequences, but she could not stop. She owed Janice at least this much. She would find Charlie.

Hours had passed with no sign of her niece, and, exhausted, Joan sat heavily on a cushioned ottoman. Each floor had the same configuration with an ottoman a small table and a mirror that rested opposite the bank of elevators. It was so similar, that she had lost track of what floor she was on, having taken the stairs as her search took her from floor to floor. The building had grown increasingly busy as the night had passed and morning arrived, it was her only sign that time had passed.

"Why, Miss, would you mind answering a question for me?"

The voice was kindly and warm, so kindly and warm in fact that Joan couldn't help but choke back a brief sob before covering her face by looking at the floor and fiddling with her hair for a moment. After she had composed herself, she looked up at the stranger whose countenance softened immediately. "I'm sorry, it's been a long day, perhaps someone else can help you?" Joan's voice was thin with a slight waver as she tried to keep her emotions in check.

"Oh my, is this the woman I met only a day or so ago? From the department store? I'm sorry, but I believe I never got your name." Joan blinked in surprise as she lifted her eyes to the oddly familiar face of the old decorator. How strange to find him here in her building. She knew she should have been at least offended, but somehow his presence was exactly what she needed. For so many years she had lived in relative isolation. Her work schedule made it impossible to meet new people, and the added responsibility of caring for the girls had closed off any hope she had of maintaining friendships. In the ensuing years after taking the girls in, she had poured everything she had into them. And now this.

The older man seemed nearly as surprised as her as he mentioned the chance meeting that felt like such a long time ago. "I... I..." Joan looked harder at the man she saw before her. He wore an old sports coat now, but there was no mistaking that kindly face.

For a moment, she sought her mind for his name. "Rupert... it was Rupert, wasn't it? I mean, Mr. Kerstman?" It was such an odd name, and she was genuinely surprised that she remembered it.

A smile bloomed on the older man's face. "Well, this must look very bad indeed, as though I were following you around, but I hope you know that this is purely the most astonishing of coincidences," the older man replied. He lifted his hand, motioning to the space beside her. "Would you mind if I sat for a moment? I'm afraid these old bones are not as youthful as they once were, and I've been walking the building quite a bit this morning."

Joan moved over to give him room, her own thinking now completely fogged. Deep inside, she felt something tickle at her mind, like a warning bell alerting her that she should have been much more worried about being surprised by this man. Yet, his mannerisms placed her at ease. Shaking the alarms away, she waited for him to take a seat, noting how light he must be, given how little his weight shifted the cushion they now shared. "Well, I can't imagine why anyone would want to walk around in here," she mentioned, realizing immediately that she was doing just that. "Say, you haven't seen a little girl, have you?"

"Oh, you mean Charlie?" he responded inquisitively.

She was taken aback at his remembering her niece's name, but then recalled that she had mentioned Charlie when they first met. Clearly this man's mind was anything but old. "Yes, Charlie, I guess you wouldn't know what she looked like, but she seems to have run off."

"My dear, I'm so sorry. I have seen a few children about, but they were with their own families. Perhaps you could give me a description and I could help you look?" Again, his voice was warm and kind and seemingly filled with authentic concern.

"No, no, this isn't your problem, I wouldn't want to trouble you. But if you do see a young girl, she's eleven with dark hair and normally very shy." Joan paused a moment as she pulled herself to her feet, feeling somewhat refreshed. "I need to be looking again. I'm on the forty-third floor, and... my name is Joan, Joan Willard-Stewart. If you see her..." She paused again as the old man stood to his feet and eyed her with growing concern.

"Absolutely. I will keep my eyes open for your young Charlie. I'm sure she's alright. I just have a feeling." With this, he smiled as he lifted a hand with a finger in the air, "And, Ms. Willard-Stewart, I do hope things go better for you."

"Thank you, Mr. Kerstman. Good day." And with that, Joan headed for the stairs and the next floor below.

Chapter 24

Adeline stood on the edge of the massive stump, her lean form silhouetted by the towering trees of the Great Wood that circled the remains of the immense tree. Above, the pale light of an orange moon cast ominous shadows over the scene in the perpetual twilight that had gripped the land since the felling of the tree whose stump she now stood atop. Adeline surveyed the gathering of Woodlings that had responded to her summons. They were so few now. The deer, of course, and the otters and beavers were always loyal to the forest and the ancient code. The smaller creatures as well as the leaders of the Flight of the Forest were gathered on the lower limbs of the surrounding trees to be better able to see her. It was the absences that worried her most. The bears, wolves, and even the great cats were missing. This was not a good sign. The split between her and Millicent was now complete, and Adeline feared that this move toward war may well end what little remained of this once vibrant community. The blight had not yet reached them, and yet it was winning.

"We knew this moment would come." Adeline's voice carried well and drew the assembly to a quiet hush. "We knew this moment would come but did not do enough to prevent it." This statement drew low murmurs from those who had gathered. "Long have the Woodlings stood against dangers that would tear our forest down. We have fought the blight with everything we have and held it at bay." It was in fact this very struggle that had contributed most to the dwindling numbers, creatures tired of facing a foe they could not see and now eager for some other solution.

"You know as well as I that Millicent has been at work, attempting to re-awaken the Ancient Powers." This was received with nods all around. Millicent and her minions had been recruiting heavily for many cycles now. They had preached about an alternative to the fight against the blight, which had first appeared after the first opening of a portal to Maridil, the first and largest of the outworlds to be discovered. Millicent believed that she could raise the Ancient Powers and control them to use against the blight, that holding to the ancient ways was simply not enough. Adeline believed differently. After months of investigation, she was now certain that the Ancient Powers were likely behind the blight, using its destructive powers to divide the Woodlings, as it indeed had. In fact, mounting evidence of the outworlder invasion suggested that the Ancient Powers might in fact have invited the outworlders as a means to restore the power and influence they once wielded.

"Millicent now has what she needs, what she has been seeking. The outworlders of Maridil have returned, and this time, they have brought with them what we feared... an heir. Even now, I am told that she prepares to call the Ancient Powers at the Place of Stones... and offer this heir as a sacrifice. If she does so, she will unleash catastrophe on us all." All were silent around her now.

Adeline allowed the silence to settle deeply before continuing. "It is true that our numbers now are small. If Millicent is able to accomplish what she seeks, we may be too few to stand against her and those who have gone to her side." Adeline began to walk slowly at the edge of the stump now.

"But we are the Woodlings of Eridul. We are bound to this forest. This is our home. For uncounted cycles, we and our ancestors have tended these trees and stood against every power that threatened." She turned back toward them, rage filling her voice now. "Only once has one of our own turned against the Forest." In saying this, she stomped a hoof on the Great Stump which had been created that day when the Mother tree had been cut down.

"We are few. But we are determined. We are few, but we will stand together. We are few! But we will rally this day to stand against this evil. We are few! But we are the Forest... And the Forest is ours!"

At this, the whole group repeated, "The Forest is ours!"

"To the Place of Stones! To stop this madness! We are the Forest! And The forest is ours!"

Again, cries arose from the Woodlings as they turned as one and began to make their way to the Place of Stones with speed.

In moments, Adeline was alone as silence now hung heavy over the Great Stump. "We are few. Too few I fear," she said softly before leaping off and chasing after the others.

Chapter 25

"Stay back you two!" urged Old Pete who lofted a wing as if to shelter Mift and Salizar as he turned to face the opening of the cave.

"What is it?" chirped Salizar as he fluttered up into the air to catch a glimpse of the cave now that Pete's bulbous shape was blocking his view.

"Daaaaare you… Daaaaare yoooooooo," added Mift as she scampered down from the boulder she had been sitting on and sprinted through the brush, appearing on top of another rock just to the side of the cave's entrance.

With a lengthy slurp, Old Pete scooped up a mouthful of water from the small pool and slowly stumped his way toward the cave. "I fink I she shomfing" he gurgled as water sloshed from his brimming beak. And with that, he arched back, drawing air through his nostrils, and blew a tremendous stream of water toward the mouth of the cave, which unsettled a wooden beam that had been propping up a large wooden barrel, which in turn tipped and then dumped the entirety of its contents down the shaft of the cave.

"Hah!" trumpeted Pete proudly as he danced from one wide foot to the next. "Let's see them survive that! Can't sneak up on Old Pete, no sir." Mift and Salizar looked on anxiously for what might come next.

Chapter 26

Jeremy and Charlie had been traveling steadily upward for some time now, and Charlie was beginning to think that they were actually going to escape this dreadfully dark cave.

"I think I see light ahead, Jeremy," Charlie noted with delight as the first dim rays of light began to filter into the cave. A light breeze had also begun to blow sweet warm air into the dampness around them.

"Ah, yes," said Jeremy brightly, "I believe we are about to be free of this place... but wait... I hear something..."

Even as he was saying this, a deluge of water filled the cavern nearly to the top, lifting both of them off their feet and tossing them like sticks along with the torrent in a tumble back down the cave. It was only with Jeremy's heroic effort in throwing out his large wings against either side of the shaft and grabbing Charlie with one foot that they managed not to be sent all the way back into the depths of the cavern.

After several moments, the water flow subsided, and Jeremy and Charlie, now soaked, managed to get back to their feet with a shake and sputter.

"What... what was that?" choked Charlie as she coughed water from her lungs. She could only imagine how she looked now with her nightgown stained and drenched. She took a moment to wring water from the garment as she regained her feet.

"Jeremy does not know. There is no waterfall this way, there is no stream of which I am aware. This is very strange, perhaps we should be careful." This said, the pair of them made their way back up the sloping path and at long last into the mouth of the cave, Charlie blinking even in the dim light of the twilight sky.

Chapter 27

"Now you strangers don't make another move!" cried out Old Pete as he lofted both wings and fluffed his feathers in an attempt to intimidate anyone or anything that might be emerging from the cave. "Old Pete has plenty more where that came from!"

Charlie had just emerged from the mouth of the cave, following behind Jeremy as she caught sight of the surprisingly large bird dancing about in front of them. While Charlie was not tall, she was still a head taller than either Jeremy or this new creature, and after everything she had been through, she was not about to be bullied by yet another strange creature.

Placing both hands on her hips, she squared her shoulders in reply. "Now wait right there, mister parrot. I'm tired, I'm cold, and now I'm all wet. And I just want to wake up from this terrible dream. I don't have any plans to hurt you or anyone else, but I will not be bullied." This time, she felt quite proud of herself for the sternness in her voice, and then she caught sight of the familiar little bird and chipmunk who had stolen her locket.

"And you two again!" She glared and pointed a finger at the pair of Mift and Salizar, who both skittered backward under her withering gaze.

"Very bright... very bright?" offered Mift sheepishly as she ducked low behind a mound of snow that covered the top of the rock she had selected for her vantage point.

"Well now," replied Pete, fluffing his feathers as much as he could before hopping backward and then up onto the rim of rocks surrounding the small open space. "This is my home, you little soft skin! You have no right to be here, so don't be getting yourself all high and mighty. Why, look at yourself. You look terrible. Good folk know how to keep better care of their feathers than that," he puffed himself up again, seemingly unfazed by her outburst.

At this proclamation, Charlie's eyes dropped to her soiled nightgown, and in the dim but better lighting of the twilight sky, she saw that it was well and truly ruined. Mud and dirt had deeply stained the entire nightgown, the nightgown that Cassie had worn and given her on the day she left. "Oh no..." she gasped involuntarily.

"There, see!" Pete trumpeted with an odd sounding bark of triumph. "And meddling with a bat as well! Why everyone knows you can't trust a bat... Why, I should hand you over to Lieutenant Stone and be done with you." At this, Old Pete hopped back down from the rocks, weaving his head back and forth at the girl.

Jeremy slumped dejectedly at the old bird's bullying, but Salizar the small finch flittered its way up and between the two groups, managing to hover in a herky jerky motion as it attempted to address them all.

"Now listen here..." Salizar began tentatively, before shaking and puffing his feathers as if pushing away some lingering restraining instinct. "All of us... just need to take a deep breath." Jeremy took in a deep breath and held it, causing Salizar to look about and reply with evident frustration in his voice. "Not literally take a deep breath, it's just a saying." The little bird alighted on the ground between all of the parties.

"Well then, little lunch snack," replied Pete. "If you're going to be in charge now, you're doing a terrible job. You've got the little soft skin and the stinky bat nearly in tears." Pete harrumphed and flapped his wings slowly, chest swelling.

"Hey there! Heeeeeeeyyyyyy there!" snapped Mift as she scampered from her spot to join her friend in the center... a stern look on her face. The diminutive creature fixed her bright eyes on each member of the small group in turn. When she had everyone's attention, she nodded to Salizar to continue, adding a satisfied, "Hey there."

Charlie could have sworn that the little bird smiled in appreciation of his companion's assistance as he turned first toward her, "We are all very sorry that you have been so badly treated. Our home is normally a wonderful place, but I'm afraid that terrible things are happening now. Your locket has been taken, and it is being used to bring a dangerous power back... one that will likely destroy all of us. We need your help, I'm afraid."

Salizar then turned to Jeremy and to Pete in turn. "We need all of your help. All of us need each other, and we need to work together."

With this, Salizar flittered into the air in front of Pete. "Great Pete, we need you to raise the Stone Army. You are the only one who can do it."

With a shrug, Old Pete let his feathers droop and dropped his wings. He let out a long sigh before sitting heavily on the ground. "Actually, little fella. That one is the only one who can raise the Stone Army." In saying this, the large bird lifted a wing to point in the direction of Charlie, to everyone's surprise.

With all falling silent around her, Charlie released her grip on the ruined nightgown and returned the unwavering gaze of the large parrot-like bird as he pointed his wing directly at her. "What? Me? How can I possibly raise an army? I'm just... I'm nobody."

Chapter 28

M s. Filmore had not needed to visit this building for several years but remembered its plain walls well. Each floor was decorated with the minimal industrial drab required of such places. Upon arriving at the forty-third floor, the social worker took note of the dilapidated state of things. While the building manager had appeared interested in taking her directly to the apartment in question himself, Ms. Filmore ushered him brusquely back onto the elevator and was now free to make her inspection with fresh eyes. The first thing she noticed was that the carpet was completely worn away down the center of the hallway, and the air tasted stagnant and musty.

Apartment forty-three twelve was just off the main corridor and about midway down a narrow hallway. Some of the doors had been papered prettily for the holiday, but this door was just bare wood. At least the lights in the hallway were all in working order.

"This is no place to raise a child," the case worker murmured to herself before knocking softly on the door.

She waited a moment and then knocked again, calling out toward the door, "Ms. Willard-Stewart? I'm here about Charlie."

Her call was followed by the unmistakable sound of interior footsteps and then a lock on the other side of the door slid clean, and the door opened a crack with the face of an older woman peering out questioningly.

"I'm sorry, Joan isn't in right now, perhaps you could come by at a different time?" Ms. Oldmire had never seen this newcomer, but her prim appearance and the briefcase in her hand could not be a good sign.

"I'm here from CPS, perhaps you can let me in, and we can wait for Joan to return?" Ms. Filmore eyed the old woman a moment longer, adding on a guess, "Ms. Oldmire, I presume?"

At the mention of her name, Ms. Oldmire stepped back, involuntarily opening the door wider before realizing what she had done. But the younger woman read it as a sign and was already gently but firmly pushing the door wider.

"I suspected as much, and I have a few questions for you as well if you have the time." The case worker could read body language well, and this woman wanted nothing more than to run, a sure sign that she would have valuable information.

"I... I don't really know anything about Charlie. I just watch the place when Joan is at work." The older woman's words were involuntarily spilling out as the caseworker's gaze took in the room. She had no intention of leaving now. "Perhaps... perhaps I could put some tea on?" Without waiting for a response, Ms. Oldmire turned quickly and made her way to the kitchen.

"Ms. Willard-Stewart... Joan," she began before correcting herself. "I mean, Joan, keeps a clean home," observed Ms. Filmore as her eyes scanned the small living space. It was indeed quite clean and tidy with a beautiful array of artwork hanging on the walls. "Quite pretty, actually... is she an artist? These paintings are beautiful."

One painting in particular caught her eye with its deep but vibrant colors depicting a resplendent forest from a bird's eye view. The detail was stunning she noted as she looked the painting over with growing interest.

Cassie's artwork was something Ms. Oldmire seemed to have no trouble talking about. Having set the water to boil, the older woman turned back around and proudly pointed to a small painted portrait that hung at the edge of the kitchen wall. "This is my favorite. It's the girls with their mother, painted from an old picture, but with so much more color than the original." Her smile faded a bit. "These were all painted by the eldest girl, Cassie."

"Yes, Cassie is in a boarding school now, right? The Governor's School, isn't that what I've heard?" Ms. Filmore was taking her time, looking at each picture in turn as she inspected the home. "Quite prestigious, and on full scholarship I understand? That's... incredibly rare." She turned back to the older woman and noted the wistful smile on her face. "You really care for these girls, don't you?"

"And for their aunt." Goldie dropped her hands along with her eyes for a moment, but when she looked back up there was steel in her gaze. "This is a good family. They've already been through so much. Please don't break them up. It... It just wouldn't be right." Emotion tinged her voice as she finished, and the whistle of the kettle gave her reason to turn away.

Waiting for the kettle whistle to die down, Ms. Filmore allowed the older woman to serve her a steaming cup of tea before responding softly, "I'm not here to break a family apart. I'm only here to make sure that Charlie is okay. Perhaps you can tell me what you know."

"Well, there isn't much to tell about the girl disappearing, but I can tell you about the three of them. I can do that." With that, Goldie nodded toward the kitchen where the two took a seat at the small table.

Chapter 29

Kraftin had never felt such power, had never imagined that such power could exist, but struggled to maintain control of his own consciousness as he swooped in strange, perilous, and impossible ways. Time itself seemed to stand still as the locket and the small moon pressed against his thickly feathered chest... burning like an iron brand. Balanced on the precipice of exhilaration and pain, the kea continued to fight against the force that seemed to have gripped him, and then, just as suddenly as it had begun, the power ceased, and Kraftin's vision clouded as he fell limply to the ground with a heavy thud.

"You outworlders know nothing." The great blue heron shook her head after she had finished etching the final symbol on the thin piece of slate. "Ah, I should have known," she commented as she stepped back to survey her work with a look of satisfaction. Kraftin, remained motionless as he watched from the ground where he had landed. The fall had knocked the wind from his chest, but he felt whole. Still, it seemed wise to wait and watch.

Gently setting the stone down in the center of the altar, Millicent walked in her stiff-legged way over to the crumpled form of the kea and with a few swift motions, unclipped the locket and the small moon, both of which had faded to a blackened shell of their former luster. Casting the locket aside, she lifted the moon for closer inspection.

"An amazing amount of power in such a small thing." This too she cast aside, turning away from the kea who remained motionless alert near one of the great monoliths that framed the interior circle. "Now, you shall behold true power!" shrieked the heron into the darkness, her voice echoing within the semi enclosed space. Her crisp cackling continued as she paced stiffly back to the center of the stone, dragging the slate slowly. Kraftin watched as Millicent balanced on one leg and lifted the slate with the other to better see the inscription she had just made. Breathing deeply, Millicent closed her eyes as she emitted a strange gurgling hum. As she did so, the crystal talon holding the thin piece of slate began to glow. As her strange chanting increased, the shadows around her grew darker, beginning to swirl in time with her tone as the sound of approaching thunder began to groan overhead.

Then the heron threw back her head, her voice crackling with energy as she chanted the verses that Kraftin presumed she had just scripted from his aerial display.

> *Thunder from the darkness,*
> *Fires from the deep,*
> *Powers that are Ancient,*
> *Awaken from your sleep.*
> *Within these ancient stones,*
> *Your promise you must keep,*
> *Your powers now I claim!*
> *My enemies to defeat!*
> *This vessel you shall fill,*
> *The ritual is complete!*

Thunder roared and echoed above the structure as the air swirled into a vortex of darkness, with Millicent at its epicenter. A deafening crack tore through the cacophony as the stone altar upon which Millicent stood split, and she lifted into the air with wings outspread, at first floating and then spiraling up into the storm.

A deep rumble shook the ground, upending the earth in response to her summons as the rocks began to split apart and the sound of great drums and horns filled the sky. Kraftin lurched involuntarily as a deep sonorous song boomed forth from a phalanx of massive stone creatures that began to emerge all around the stone circle, tearing up trees by their roots as Millicent's cackling laugh was punctuated by bursts of immense war horns. Clearly forgotten now, Kraftin rolled from his side to the edge of the vortex where he huddled within the shadows of the stone structure, transfixed by the power he saw before him.

Strokes of lightning filled the sky, illuminating the scene with pulsing strobes of blinding light. Kraftin could clearly hear Millicent's voice shaking the trees as she ordered her minions to war.

"To the Great Stump! Where I shall call the Ancient Powers and bend them to my will. We shall no longer cower like lesser beings— we shall be ascendant!" Her cackle echoed as she took flight with slow, but powerful downstrokes.

As the heron lifted away and the sound of horns and howls filled the night sky, Kraftin shook the dust from his feathers as he emerged from the shadows. A dim metallic gleam caught his eye, pulling his gaze to the burnt locket and then the small moon that Millicent has recently discarded. The moon he picked up with a taloned claw, inspecting it closely.

"So, the witch was using me... well, two can play this game. But carefully now. I must find Marvelous. The master was right about this place. There is power here." Seeing that the small moon appeared to be devoid of its power, he tossed it aside. His talons and his wits would have to serve him now. With that thought, the powerful bird lifted himself into the air, wheeling to the east where Marvelous had last been sent. "Enjoy this while it lasts, Millicent. This power you have will soon be mine."

Ambush

Chapter 30

The day was bright, and the air was crisp as Brian made his way back to Building fourteen, but he took none of it in. The funk from the night before had simply soured in his stomach so that even the cheery glint of the sun on the glass as it reflected a beautiful blue sky could not cut through his gloom. Brian was angry. He was angry with himself, angry with Jinx, angry with Kettle, and angry with this dead-end job. Thus was his mood as he shoved his way into the building and stumped his way to the maintenance office on the first floor.

The day crew had already come and gone it seemed, which was for the better. By design, Brian worked rotating shifts to maximize building relationships across his team, and this week he was on the later schedule, though he still arrived earlier than required to organize for the day. But Brian had little time to himself before the door creaked open, and in sauntered the last face on earth he needed to see, that of Jinx January.

"Did you hear the news!" The slight man chirped in an overly cheery way.

Brian glared at him.

"Oh my. Grumpy today, aren't we? Well, I can certainly understand why. But you're a big boy, you'll survive," Jinx trailed off, smiling while observing Brian's darkening countenance before continuing. "The building is abuzz today! Seems that Ms. Filmore from CPS is turning the building inside out. She's here investigating that woman on the forty-third who lost her child." Jinx prattled on as if Brian weren't even there. The man was clearly oblivious. Just an underling who shouldn't get under his skin, but Brian couldn't stand the sight of the slight man at the moment. "CPS?" he responded dryly, if for no other purpose than to shut the other man up.

"Child protective services, of course," smiled Jinx as he took a seat on a stool near the workbench. "Goodness, man, you do live under a rock, don't you? Well... somehow..." here Jinx lingered on the word before repeating it conspiratorially, "somehow, word got out that one of the building residents lost their child. Can you imagine? Lost their child. Well, the minute I discovered that, it was my duty to alert the authorities." Jinx was cut short by Brian's response.

"Who? What child?" Brian jerked around, suspicion filling his voice.

"Oh, the little girl in forty-three twelve... very sad story really. I'm just glad I could act in time. Wouldn't want to be in the shoes of her aunt, they'll probably have to take the child away. It's better that way really." Jinx's voice was almost gleeful as he gloried in the drama he'd been able to generate off of a simple rumor.

For a moment, Brian searched his memory, trying to recall where he had heard the numbers before. And then it came to him in a flash as he blurted out, "Joan? You turned in Joan?" Anger was rising again, and this time he just didn't care. In a moment, he had taken the smaller man by the lapels, nearly lifting him off the ground as he snarled into his face, "You turned in Joan... why, you filthy little man."

With that, he shoved Jinx away. The smaller man nearly toppled to the ground, but caught himself hard against the door, shock registering on his face, but it was quickly replaced by a stern and knowing grin.

"You'll pay for that, Brian... you can't just manhandle me. I'll tell Kettle about this. You can be sure."

Composing himself, Jinx backed away cautiously, appearing to be alert for any other physical threats from the larger maintenance chief. "And you can forget Joan and her little girl. They'll be gone before the week is out. This isn't a fairytale, Brian... this is life."

Brian only barely held himself back this time, and instead pushed Jinx through the door before slamming it shut to keep himself from doing anything more incredibly foolish than what he had just done.

Chapter 31

"Halt! Halt!" The voice of Adeline cut through the rumbling sound of the Woodling host as they rolled as one through the Great Forest toward the Place of Stones. As the forward line drew to an unsteady and impatient halt, Adeline directed her senses forward, instinct telling her that something was wrong.

A muted horn blared from one of her lieutenants, bringing the rest of the Woodling host to a halt some paces behind the front line. Slowly, all returned to silence in the surrounding wood. This day, like all the rest, had dawned in the perpetual gloom of twilight as the moon remained hidden behind a layer of clouds and the thick forest canopy above. Tiny specks of snow filtered through the canopy above on their lazy, errant path to the forest floor which stretched white and undisturbed before them.

"Something is wrong, Jericho." Adeline had just turned toward her lieutenant, a thickly muscled bull moose who towered over her and the others around them. She was about to issue a command when the ground beneath them began to rumble. A tremor shook the ground beneath the Woodlings, breaking open steaming fissures along the forest floor in front of them. Adeline looked to her lieutenant, about to say something, but the ground around them split as well, erupting in geysers of dirt and rock, tossing the towering trees from side to side as thick tendrils of misty darkness seeped from the broken ground to engulf the Woodlings in an inky, choking mist. The sound of monstrous horns filled the air, punctuated by the resounding concussive boom of colossal drums that sent tremors through the ground with each impact.

"Pull back! Pull back!" Adeline commanded.

But her shout was too late as the whole Woodling line was beset by the wolf pack, who leapt from the shadows around them, tearing into the front line with wild eyes and foaming mouths. Adeline reared instinctively, a hoof barely deflecting the dark, leaping form of a wolf who quickly bounded away and approached again in a low and growling stance.

"Adeline!" hissed Ferris, the wolf pack commander. "I warned you this day would come." The lean gray wolf circled slowly, her yellow eyes focused intently on Adeline, both threatening and wary.

"What have you done, Ferris... Millicent is mad with power, this will destroy the forest, destroy all of us... even you." Adeline lowered her head and lashed at the wolf with her spiraling horns before leaping backward in retreat to the sound of the wolf's chuckling, barking laughter. Ferris lunged again, sharp white fangs flashing, but Adeline's swift movement parried the beast aside at the last moment. Adeline knew that if she engaged one on one, the Woodlings would scatter. She must get them to a defensible position before all was lost.

"Retreat! Retreat to the Great Stump! Retreat!" Adeline's voice was nearly drowned out by the growing sounds of battle all around as more dark shapes joined the wolves in the attack. It was an ambush. Somehow, Millicent had completed her dark task and advanced toward the Great Stump far more rapidly than Adeline had thought possible. Worse, Adeline knew the sound of those great blaring horns. Could Millicent have actually managed to call the Stone Army to her side? If that were the case, then all was truly lost.

"You are finished, Adeline! Run if you will, but you cannot hide! Millicent has summoned the Ancient Powers, and she is coming for you!" sneered the wolf at the retreating Adeline before shaking off the sting from the Adeline's raking antlers and pouncing on the nearest Woodling with a snarl followed by a long howl. As if in response, the whole wolf pack joined her in a rising, ghostly howling as they attacked and pushed the Woodlings back toward the Great Stump.

"She may have the Stone Army, but she doesn't have the Ancient Powers yet... And she won't if I can help it," breathed Adeline as she turned and leapt away with her retreating forces. They would have to rally now by the Great Stump and somehow find a way to hold there. Adeline and her forces crashed back along the path they had just come, now in full retreat with Millicent's host in pursuit.

Following near the back of her army, Millicent spread her wings wide as if to embrace the darkness that rolled before her. An aura of twisting green flames licked about her as she cackled into the darkness, flapping her wings to send more twisting tendrils ahead of her. All around, the forest withered, leaving a dark trail of death in her wake.

"Come, my children! Come with me to claim the prize that is ours!" Her shriek was electric in the swirling darkness. Even the leaves of the most impressive trees withered away at her approach. "Now... Rise, titans of the earth! Rise! I command you, children of Azilem! Rise and follow me."

As she floated forward, the ground around her tore apart as numerous hulking stone shapes crawled from the ground, gashing the vegetation as they did. Their deep thundering steps gouged deep chunks from the forest floor as they advanced slowly with the heron and her teeming hoard. Inexorably, the calamitous host progressed toward the Great Stump.

"There will be no Stone Army to save you this time, Adeline… not this time… for it is mine!" Her cackling laughter was now punctuated by the resounding boom of drums and blare of horns. Indeed, the spectacular Stone Army of legend and lore had risen to her call.

As the dark host roared and crashed their way forward, a lone stone creature dug its way from the ground as well. This one was much smaller than the others, and its coal black eyes bore a hint of intellect unlike the other lumbering beasts. Comprised of what appeared to be an animated jumble of smooth river rocks, the small officer stretched an arm forward. The rocks and pebbles of the forest floor vibrated in response.

"We shall see about that, Millicent… We shall see," the Lieutenant muttered as it watched its golem brethren move forward with the advancing throng. As its outstretched arm dropped, the rocks along the forest floor grew still. With a nod of satisfaction, the Stone Lieutenant turned and made its way back to the Place of Stones, for it had work to do before all was lost.

Chapter 32

"I say... you are quite rash for a soft skin," intoned Pete as he stumped his way behind the small group through a winding trail with Mift in the lead. "You do realize that the Stone Army has not fought in cycles upon cycles? Probably aren't any of them even awake now." The large bird had a funny loping walk that drew a smile to Charlie's face. While his demeanor was gruff, Charlie had come to enjoy the old creature's company.

"If you don't mind me asking..." added the fruit bat as it trailed in an awkward loping shuffle behind Pete. "What exactly is the Stone Army?" Jeremy had remained relatively quiet since exiting the cave, and in the light, Charlie could see long ugly welts across his wings, which he held tightly to his back. Those might have been caused by the ropes that bound him in the cave, but instinct told her that Jeremy had been treated poorly during his captivity.

"Now THAT, my stinky fellow, is the best thing you've asked all day... might actually be the only thing you've asked all day," answered Pete ponderously as he loped along.

"Why, the Stone Army has saved the forest more than once from all manner of dangers," Salizar chimed in after alighting on a limb just ahead of the trio. "It is the greatest fighting force in the realm and has never seen defeat!" he chirped happily.

"Daaaaare you... Daaaaare yoooooooo..." puffed Mift from the lead of the group as if to support Salizar's assessment. While Charlie felt that she should still be angry at the small pair, she found them both so endearing as to wonder why she had not followed them from the beginning. Sullenly, the thought struck her that much of this may have been avoided had she just trusted them. Trust was such a strange thing, only seeming obvious after the fact.

"Oh right.... Right you are, however, it has not always been used on behalf of the forest. You might say its history is... complicated." countered Old Pete as he trudged along. "The Stone Army is as ancient as the very ground you walk upon... the original defenders of the whole realm. But some say they were originally created to serve Azilem."

"Those are just silly stories told to scare the young ones," countered Salizar with a sour tone to his tweeting reply. "But, I have heard that they follow the orders of their master, no matter who that may be." Salizer grew thoughtful then, flittering off in a long loop through the trees.

"True, true. But they are impressive! Some of them stand as tall as the great shaggy elephants of the north! And taller!" Old Pete let out that strange barking call of his once again as he began swinging his wings from side to side in a mimic of the creatures he must be referring to.

Charlie couldn't help herself, giggling at the sight of the old parrot-like creature waddling along. She continued to warm to these fascinating new friends. "So, are they asleep then?" she asked before adding, "I guess they must be if we have to wake them."

"Why, my dear, they do not sleep like you or I," intoned the old kakapo. "There is a mystical force that binds the Stone Army to the very bedrock of this realm. Deep within the ground, there is said to be an enormous stone kingdom where the army dwells. When the prince of that kingdom is summoned by the true heir of the realm it is bound to send a tenth of its mightiest warriors to their aide, to be commanded by the legendary Stone Lieutenant." Old Pete's gait had grown even more grandiose as he spoke, if that were possible.

"Yes, Charlie... they are asleep and need to wake up," added Salizar as he swooped quietly back to the group and alighted on an overhanging branch.

"Just wake up! Juuuuust wake up!" added Mift from the front of the group.

Charlie giggled again and nodded knowingly toward Salizar but straightened her face when she noticed that the kakapo was giving the little finch a hard stare.

With a sniff and another odd barking cough, Old Pete continued, "I have only seen the Stone Army once... way back when I was but a small hatchling... and even then, I was bigger than this little yellow snack." Pete hopped abruptly toward the little finch, causing Salizar to flutter into the air, drawing a satisfied look to the kakapo's owl-like face.

"So, how do we... wake them up... exactly?" queried Charlie as she hid a grin and continued following after Mift along the trail.

"Well now, all we need is the key," replied Pete.

"Yes, about that..." twittered Salizar. "It appears that the key may have been... misplaced."

"What! Well, celestial stones, that won't do! That won't do at all!" trumpeted the kakapo. "How could you lose the most important artifact to enter the realm in more than a thousand cycles?" he stammered, thumping a foot to the ground while fluffing his wings wide in a show of frustration and amazement.

Charlie's hand fell absently to her pocket where the missing locket had once been and instinctively felt that this must be her fault. "Oh... was my.... Was my locket the key?" Her voice tightened as her eyes shifted to the ground, already knowing the answer.

"It... it... it sounds as though it may have been. But we can find another way, Charlie. There's always another way," intoned the fruit bat before stepping quickly to the side of the trail as the kakapo surged forward in a flurry, just missing knocking Jeremy over in the process.

"You say you lost it? Why then, we need to mount a search at once and get it back! The key... the key is everything!" Old Pete fluffed his large chest out, attempting to reach the girl's height. Failing to do so, he stepped back so as not to have to look directly up at her. "You're certainly a careless little soft skin, aren't you?" Pete harrumphed.

"Well I... I didn't know..." answered Charlie defensively. She cast her eyes across the group, landing on Jeremy in the end, who merely shrugged, but smiled back supportively.

"We know, we know, it's alright, Charlie," replied the finch in a soothing whistle. "Mift and I last saw your locket at the Place of Stones... and that is where we're heading now. I'm sure we can find it... Mift and I can find anything." Salizar sounded simultaneously confident and fretful.

"But, there might be another one." repeated Jeremy in his soft tones.

"What do you mean... another one," queried Old Pete as he stumped back toward the bat and leaned his big beak into Jeremy's face. "Are you saying you have seen the second key? Preposterous! It was destroyed." Old Pete spoke this last with a note of finality.

"Well, if it is a locket from our world, one of the companions that accompanied me... the mean one... He wore a locket around his neck." As Old Pete approached, Jeremy had continued backing away from until he bumped up against the trunk of a tree with a grunt.

"Impossible. Outrageous. Unthinkable I tell you." Pete turned away from Jeremy and returned to the trail as he continued. "If the second key existed… and If it were somehow here at the same time as the first key… well…"

"That would mean the end of us all… for with both keys, one could unlock the gates of Stone Kingdom itself… and even call upon the Ancient Powers though it would take the Celestial Star to command them." Salizar had settled on the ground in the middle of the trail. "But as Pete has said… that is impossible."

"Daaaaare youuuuu… Dare you…. Dare you…" Mift warned softly as the party stepped out of the brush onto a small ridge that overlooked a sloping clearing that led to a circle of massive standing stones.

"Oh my… What happened here?" wondered Old Pete as he pushed his way to the front of the group and peered down at the sight before them.

Chapter 33

Still seething from his recent encounter with Jinx, Brian decided to take the stairs as a way to blow off some steam, but the long climb just made his legs ache. Having soldiered all the way to the tenth floor, he exited the emergency stairwell and stepped into the dimly lit service hall, making his way to the clipboard hanging near the door.

"Lights in 1012, 1015, and 1024. Filters… pretty much everywhere," Brian muttered while reading through the task list. "Might as well fix something while I'm here," he noted wearily while pushing the door open and stepping into the residential hallway. The dark carpeting was worn smooth down the center, and the air smelled of must, dust, and old cigarette smoke. This building had never really seen better days.

The sound of a door closing pulled his eyes to a turn in the corridor just in time to see a familiar yet forlorn looking face walking toward him. It was Joan. She looked exhausted, haggard, and frail, her eyes cast to the floor. She looked the very picture of dejection and a fitting muse to the dilapidated corridor that framed her.

"Joan?" The words were out of his mouth before he could think, but the woman lifted her eyes at the mention of her name and offered a worn smile.

"Oh, good. I needed to see you anyway." Joan picked up her pace just a bit to cover the distance between them. She was holding a photo in one hand and a cell phone in the other.

"If it's about the air vents, I'll try to get up there today. I just haven't had the chance yet." Brian's mind was racing with the horrible news he had just uncovered in his confrontation with Jinx.

"What?" she responded looking confused. "Oh, the other day. No. No. I'm not worried about the vents. It's Charlotte. She seems to have wandered off."

Immediately, Brian's heart sank, remembering Jinx's words, which colored his next remarks. "Oh. About that. Seems like the whole tower is talking about it." Again, Brian tried to think of a way to tell Joan about Jinx calling Child Protective Services, but each phrase that came to mind was worse than the last.

Joan froze nearly in mid step, a sudden lost expression swept across her countenance.

"What? Why? Charlie's only been missing... how could anyone..." Her voice trailed off as the realization must have struck her like a wave crashing ashore. "Oh no. I've been searching door to door on every floor since she went missing. I've told everyone. Of course, of course..." Joan's voice faded as she cast her eyes to her hands. The photo she held was now shaking like a leaf in an autumn breeze.

Brian didn't know what to do, but instinctively he placed a hand on her shoulder, giving her a few moments of silence. When he responded at last, his voice was low and level. "I'll help you find her. I have a team, and we can help. I'm sorry we didn't do something sooner." He could feel her trembling under his hand but felt powerless in the moment.

Joan looked to be lost in a replay of every discussion she'd had since the night before. Brian knew the feeling all too well as he had been replaying his conversation with Jinx over and over. "Of course. Everyone knows because I told them," Joan repeated as her eyes bore into the photo in her hand. This wasn't the first time Brian had witnessed the effects of shock, but this felt personal.

"Joan. It will be alright, but I think you should head back to your apartment." Brian didn't want to break the news he'd just learned from Jinx, but she needed to know that Child Services had already been in the building, that they might be waiting for her in her apartment.

"Yes... Yes, thank you, Brian. I may as well just keep going. If everyone is talking about it, then someone is bound to find her." She was about to turn away when Brian interrupted. Clearly she was not taking his hint.

"Child Protective Services was called early this morning. Someone has already been in the building. They may have sent someone to your apartment. I'm sorry, Joan, but I think you should go back to your apartment." His voice trailed off as he felt her shock register through his hand, which he lifted quickly from her shoulder.

"What? Why... Child Services? That doesn't make any sense... she just ran off for a few hours... she's never done anything like that before... are you... are you sure?" Brian knew it to have been more than a few hours. If Jinx had gotten word and had time to call in the service worker—they responded quickly, but not that quickly.

"The building manager Jinx, err, Jonathan January told me himself. Joan, you should get back to your apartment. I'll look for Charlie. I won't stop until I've found her, and I know this building well. I have access to camera feeds. If she's here, I'll find her." Brian wished he could do something, anything to comfort her, but he simply had no words as his own mind filled again with rage at the duplicitous Jinx.

Joan turned away in a haze. Somehow she was walking, at least she could see her own feet moving and then stopping just as the elevator bell rang and the doors slid open. Brian was there, holding the door for her and pushing the button for the forty-third floor. He must have said something else as the doors closed, but Joan was numb. The world was a blur. "They can't take her from me. That doesn't make any sense. I'm not a bad mother. We're just… It's just hard right now." She kept repeating this phrase, mumbling it over and over as her feet carried her forward.

Joan could feel tears cresting in her eyes but shook them down when the elevator doors slid open as she arrived on her floor. And then she was running, running down the hall toward her apartment, and as she rounded the corner, she breathed a sigh of relief at finding the hallway empty. Abruptly, the door to her apartment opened and out stepped Ms. Oldmire, who caught sight of her and immediately met her in the hallway, taking her by the elbow and ushering her into the apartment before closing the door.

"She's gone now, Joan." Ms. Oldmire's voice was quavering as she spoke. "She'll be back I'm sure. I did what I could. But I'm just… I'm so sorry." Ms. Oldmire's voice resounded like a dull buzz as Joan collapsed onto the couch and wept.

Chapter 34

"I didn't know we ordered a decorator this year." Jinx was strolling into the tall building lobby as he came upon an older man, primly dressed, standing on a ladder, and stringing gold ribbon around a surprisingly good-looking tree. As the older man turned toward him, Jinx couldn't help but smile. Even the residue of his recent clash with Brian dimmed under this keen man's gaze. He reminded Jinx of an old man that used to sell roasted nuts on the corner of the street he grew up on. Indeed, the return of that specific memory shocked Jinx.

"Why, Jonathan, I believe, is it not?" the older man replied, carefully stepping down from the small ladder before brushing his hands together and offering one toward Jinx in a friendly gesture. "Kerstman. Rupert Kerstman at your service." The man held his hand out for a moment longer but dropped it as Jinx made no move to return the gesture.

"Oh, I'm sorry. I don't really do that. Germs and all this time of year." Jinx looked about before dropping his voice conspiratorially, adding, "Sickness spreads quickly through this tower, you just can't ever be too careful."

"I've always found that the warmth of an authentic greeting can dispel any manner of ills no matter how dark or dreary a situation may seem." While it seemed impossible, the man's smile broadened as his eyes peered deeply into Jinx's own, uncomfortably so.

Drawing a smile on his face, Jinx forced his gaze away, turning from the man to the tree. "How on earth did you get this thing in here?" Jinx surprised himself with the question as it was precisely what he was thinking, which was rarely what he verbalized.

"Ah," replied the strange man with a light air and a touch of pride. "You'd be amazed what can happen when you ask for people's help. It seems that a generous donation was given to the East Side Foundation to spruce up the tenant buildings during the holiday season. I've been querying residents on a few of the floors, and it seems a tree in the lobby would face the least objection." He chuckled with this. "Funny how the holidays can be the most polarizing rather than fostering the togetherness they are intended to celebrate."

"Well. Hmmm." Jinx found himself again without a quick come back. The force of genuine goodwill from this man was nearly as powerful in its own way as that of Kettle. "Well, I'm surprised you didn't come to me first. I am the building manager after all."

"Oh, dear me. Too true," replied Kerstman. "Mr. Kettle was kind enough to give me the go ahead when I met with him earlier. But, if you feel your residents wouldn't want a tree, I'm sure I could take this elsewhere and find something more appropriate with which to brighten your lobby. Perhaps a train set?" The older man had lifted a hand to his chin as if seriously considering bringing in a train display.

"Oh no, no. If Mr. Kettle has given approval and you say the residents are happy with a tree, I wouldn't dare to get in the way." Jinx wondered again if the man were honestly thinking of putting a train in the lobby. While a bizarre thing to suggest, it was triggering additional memories of Jinx's own childish fascination with the model trains that were on frequent display this time of year.

"Come now, Jonathan. We have some funds remaining. What do you think the children in the building would most enjoy? A tree after all is pretty, but not much more than that." This Kerstman fellow was just standing there watching Jinx now.

Jinx could feel the man's entire presence without looking at him, and it was as if the weight of it was somehow squeezing into all of Jinx's thoughts and memories. Feeling a sudden urge to leave, he turned back to the older man and nodded as the mix of odd emotions rose in his throat. "Oh I, I wouldn't have any idea about that," Jinx could hear himself saying as he turned abruptly and headed out of the building for some much-needed air.

Just behind him, he could hear Kerstman offer in a quiet tone that rang in his ears, "Well. If you think of anything, Jonathan... just let me know."

Chapter 35

"I think it's time we step things up a notch, Marvelous." Kraftin's voice drifted from the trees above the great cat as Marvelous silently made his way back toward the stone monument. A flurry of wings broke the silence as the kea dropped to a rock in front of the tiger's path.

"They are all weaklings, yet we traipse around on their errands," growled the tiger as he sat back on his haunches and eyed the large bird. "You seem to have something in mind," Marvelous noted with a low and expectant growl.

"That, I do," responded the kea. "The heron is getting her power from somewhere or something. She isn't powerful on her own. That means, we just need to take whatever it is that she has."

"The crystal," pondered the tiger, recalling the crystal that was affixed to one of Millicent's talons. "She is a wary creature, though. That makes getting close all the more challenging. But not impossible." The tiger's tail swished along the ground in indication that he was envisioning the moment vividly in his mind.

"She has knowledge, but she rules with fear. If she can control the others with words and tricks, we should have no trouble making our own deals. After all, everyone wants the same things."

The kea had begun to pace back and forth, watching marvelous while relating his plan. Tilting his head from side to side for a moment, the kea added, "I've been doing some surveillance."

"Oh?" responded the tiger with interest. "And have you found the star?"

Kraftin smiled at his companion's response. Marvelous looked like a brute, for certain, but no detail escaped his notice, which was what made him such an ideal ally. "I don't think the star is anything tangible," the parrot-like bird continued. "That little locket the girl had is all burned out. No. I've noticed that there are three points that are set apart from each other like a triangle. I could feel the drafts change as I flew over the lines between them." Kraftin stabbed a talon into the snow softened ground at their feet, carving a triangular shape in illustration.

"The stone circle is one point. What are the others?" Again, the deep voice of the tiger rolled like distant thunder as it warmed to the hatching plan, having quickly surmised the significance of the place with the large stone monoliths.

Kraftin stabbed the ground at another vertex on the triangle. "The second is some sort of clearing with a large stump from a tree, a tree larger than any I have ever seen, or it once was."

The kea had spent a good bit of time calculating the precise distances between the three locations and was now certain that they were all related. Stabbing the final vertex, the kea added, "the third location is a stony mound and a series of caves... and as it happens, there is a small party, including the girl, who has somehow escaped her captivity, heading from there back to the circle of stones. I think the girl is the center of all of this. I don't know how yet, but that is what I feel."

"Then we intercept them? Taking the girl would be simple." The tiger smiled with menace as a growl grew deep in his chest.

"Oh, I think toying with them a little might be more interesting," cackled Kraftin. "But yes, the girl is the key. I don't think the heron with all her growing army can do anything further without the girl. But I think we should try to... align ourselves with the girl and her little party of misfits. We could offer a truce to gain her help in taking down the old hag."

Marvelous stood slowly, prefacing his next words with another low growl. "The girl has seen you already, you'll have to convince her you mean no harm this time."

"As it happens, that is a skill I have in abundance. And if it doesn't work, I'll have you there to just... take the girl anyway. Either way, we get what we want." With a sudden jump and a few strokes from its powerful wings, the kea lifted itself back into the trees. "They should be arriving at the stones shortly. I'll meet you there." His voice filtered down from the branches, followed by the mighty flapping of wings as Kraftin took to the skies.

The great white tiger stood silently for a moment longer, pondering the plan before turning and making his way back toward the circle of stones.

Disaster

Chapter 36

U pon cresting the ridge, the small group of companions gaped in amazement at the destruction surrounding the ancient ring of stones. While the ancient stone circle stood tall against the gloom of perpetual twilight, the surrounding forest and fields were torn and rent as though a massive host of creatures had ripped them up from the roots. A long stretch of broken ground and downed trees carved a path that led inexorably north.

Seeing no obvious sign of any other presence, the party navigated cautiously down the shallow slope from the ridge. Mift and Salizar were by far the quickest of the group, arriving first and halting outside the opening to the tomb-like chamber, or the Place of Stones, as it was known. Salizar kept to the air, making rapid sweeps of the site, but giving no indication of finding signs of other life or movement.

Charlie marveled at the ancient looking structure, wondering what kind of machines must have been used to lift such enormous stones into their upright positions. Counting eight stones in all, she could see that they were placed in a "standing" position, each one pressed against the side of the other to form an enclosed space within. Charlie estimated that the inner circle must be twice as big as her small apartment, such was the size of the enormous circling stones. The stones themselves were a weather-beaten gray in color, with a rough surface that looked as though they had been hewn by hand into their oblong shapes.

An odd thought struck Charlie as she gazed at the ancient ring— these stones looked familiar. She couldn't imagine where she might have seen something like this before, but the lingering impression remained. In any case, she didn't have long to ponder the mystery as her thoughts were immediately interrupted by a shout.

"Halt! Stay right where you are and no harm will befall you," instructed a gravelly voice as the last of the small party approached the otherwise vacant looking clearing outside the circle of stones.

"Dare you... Daaaaareeee you," retorted Mift in a sharp voice. The chipmunk suddenly appeared atop a pile of smooth stones not far from the opening of the ring of obelisks. "Dare you!" Mift repeated with emphasis, folding her arms across her chest as she thumped a foot on the smooth stone where she stood, looking about furtively.

"Mift! What... what are you doing? You'll get yourself hurt!" twittered Salizar as he continued to circle about, his fluttering pattern having taken on a frenzied pattern.

"I do declare!" added Old Pete as he fluffed his feathers and spread his wings wide while waddling into the clearing after finally catching up to the party. "Show yourself, you disembodied ghost!" he demanded with a croak.

Charlie chuckled at all of the antics, feeling more at home with this small group than she had in what felt like a very long time. "I don't see anyone. How about you, Jeremy?" she asked, casting her eyes to the bat who had remained at the back of the group, his dark fur blending into the deep shadows cast by the muted sky above.

"Well, there is plenty of noise, but I can't see anything out of place," Jeremy responded as he tilted his head this way and that. "Ah yes, there it is! The little chittery one is sitting on top of our speaker I believe." Somewhere along their journey from the caves Jeremy had found an ash limb that was both firm and straight. After plucking the leaves, he had converted the limb into a fine walking stick that he had been using to feel at the ground when his echolocation was insufficient. This, he pointed in the direction of the pile of stones upon which Mift sat.

"Hey there! Hey there!" Mift chittered as she dropped down to all fours, grabbing onto the stone which had started to rise from the ground, lifting the small chipmunk into the air. The party watched in wonder as the pile of stones began to rattle and rise from the ground, vibrating oddly as they did. Even as Mift clung to the uppermost stone, the small surrounding stones began to take shape, gathering beneath the head to form two arms, two legs, and a body.

"I said, halt!" the voice commanded once again, this time with a little more ferocity. With a final grinding lurch, the final stones snapped into place, revealing a medium sized figure standing before them, with Mift clinging to the top of its oblong head. "Not a step further. Any of you. You have entered the official territory of the Stone Army, and I, as its Lieutenant, require you to present yourselves or be utterly destroyed." This last it said so matter of factly that Charlie found herself chuckling again as the small stone creature was not much larger than she.

"Dare you!" Mift's response was sharp as the small chipmunk tapped the stone head furiously with a soft paw.

"I say, what magic is this!" inquired the Lieutenant, turning its head this way and that, nearly dislodging Mift, who clung on ferociously. "What manner of darkness do you control! I will have you know that the stone army is impervious to your inconsequential powers, so you might as well surrender now before the trouble begins." As the creature spoke, the stones that formed its arms, legs, and torso undulated and rolled about, held in place by some unseen force.

Charlie shook her head, barely holding in her mirth at the sight of the silly chipmunk dancing atop the head of this stone creature. Holding down another giggle, she strode toward the creature and came to a crisp stop, clapping both of her feet together and offering a salute like she had seen soldiers doing once in a parade. "I am Charlie, and this is my company, reporting to the stone army for orders," Charlie intoned with mock gravity. She smartly snapped her hand back to her side and smiled at the stone creature, who returned her gaze with a pair of glistening obsidian pebbles.

The creature's stone head swiveled until an etched face stared back at Charlie. The mouth appeared to move while the Lieutenant spoke, but it did so in an odd and mechanical way that seemed slightly unnatural. After all that she had seen, though, a talking stone creature seemed to fit this world quite well in Charlie's estimation. As she waited, the stone creature slowly yet skillfully returned her salute.

"That is more like it," intoned the Lieutenant. "Well, Charlie Company. As it happens, you have arrived just in time, for it seems that the rest of the army has been stolen and is currently marching north under the orders of a rather mean-looking skinny-legged blueish puff of feathers." The Stone Lieutenant's head began to rotate once again, suspended above the stones that comprised its body. As it inspected the other members of the party, its odd dark eyes stopped at each one in turn before the head spun rapidly back to view Charlie as if it were wound on a coiled spring. "Well, Charlie Company, prepare your troops for inspection! After all, every great march to battle deserves a proper inspection of the troops."

"Wait, what do you mean the rest of the army was stolen?" queried Charlie with a hint of confusion in her voice.

Old Pete had been rocking back and forth, looking at the ground, but snapped back to attention at Charlie's question. "Wait, are you telling me that you've lost the rest of the army, Lieutenant?" As if to emphasize his consternation, the large bird waddled up to stand beside Charlie, tilting his owl-like face at an angle and opening his eyes in a blatant stare. "How do you lose a whole army?" the kakapo barked, eyes blinking.

"Tish, tosh, let's not get lost in the details. All battles are fluid things after all," replied the lieutenant without a hint of worry. "But, ah! I see an old veteran has returned. Looking a bit plump around the middle aren't we, Sergeant Pete?" The stones of the Lieutenant's arm stretched out until the finger of one hand poked the bird in his admittedly soft belly. "Still not fit for aerial patrol, are we?" the lieutenant added as it leaned in toward the bird who stood just a feather or two taller.

Pete spluttered and flopped his wings over his round belly. "Blah, bleh, meh... whatever. I'm in fine fighting form and never was able to fly, as you should rightly recall," the flightless bird retorted. "All I've ever needed was my beak, legs, and wits, which are just as strong and sharp as ever." Old Pete puffed his feathers and stretched out his legs to appear a bit taller.

Not finished with its inspection, the Stone Lieutenant turned its gaze back to Charlie. "And you, Charlie Company leader. Do you have any battle experience? Any skills? Any weapons?" For the first time after rising from a pile of rubble, the Stone Lieutenant took a step, beginning a slow march around Charlie with a surprising if not rumbly grace.

"Why... of course not. I'm just a girl from the city." Charlie was all out of sorts at this point, still recovering from the shock that this stone army may not be available to them. The thought of being a central part of raising the all-important stone army had buoyed her spirits to such an extent that Charlie now felt at a loss.

"Very Bright... veeeeerrrrry bright," intoned Mift from the top of the stone creature's head where it had become quite used to the jostling.

At that moment, Salizar the finch fluttered down from the sky, clutching in its beak a blackened chain with a small dark pendant clinging to the center.

The moment that Charlie's eyes caught sight of her once beautiful necklace, her breath caught. "Oh no... is that..."

Salizar fluttered to the ground, laying the small, burned necklace and pendant at Charlie's feet before replying. "I'm afraid it is, Charlie. It seems that the key has already been used... someone has already called the Stone Army."

Chapter 37

The new day had dawned with a dreary gray sky as Joan sat at the table in her small eat-in kitchen facing the sharply dressed woman from Child Protective Services who had arrived with precise punctuality early that morning. Joan had prepared coffee and tea and baked a few muffins which sat untouched on the table between them as Ms. Filmore lifted a folder and notepad from her briefcase and set them on the table.

The click from the service officer's pen was audible in the stillness of the apartment as Joan sat on the verge of panic, clasping her hands together in an attempt to keep them from shaking.

"Ms. Willard-Stewart. Do you mind if I call you Joan?" began the woman in a professional but courteous tone.

"Uh yes… yes that would be fine," replied Joan, her voice quivering.

"Joan," the other woman began again. "I'm not here to take Charlotte away from you. I'm here to make sure that you and Charlotte have what you need, and to help determine what the best circumstances are for you and for your niece."

"Charlie is my daughter now," Joan corrected. While the adoption process had completed only a few months ago, and still stung a little when anyone referred to Charlie as anything but her daughter. "The adoption was completed about five months ago. The courts felt at the time that I could provide a suitable home for her and her sister." Joan's voice was tight with emotion as she finished the phrase with pursed lips and a furrowed brow.

"Yes. Yes, I understand." Ms. Filmore's tone softened just a hair as she watched Joan. Perhaps there was more to this caseworker than Joan had first thought. "Listen. I'm sure you've heard all the worst about the people in my profession. And I understand that this is extremely personal and threatening for you. Your... daughter... is missing. You are worried about her and want to find her, and now I'm here." The woman paused a moment before adding, "Does that about sum things up"

"Yes." The word hung in the air for a moment. "I don't think this is helpful at all... But all I want is to get Charlie back. More than anything, I just want her to be safe and happy." Joan could feel tears at the corners of her eyes along with a mix of anger and fear. Even now, local police were moving floor to floor in a complete search for Charlie. But neither they nor Brian and his team had turned up even a sign of her.

The air vent in the apartment hummed dully as the two women sat in silence. Then Joan heard the pen click again and looked slowly up at the other woman who was watching her with an unexpected hint of kindness in her eyes.

"I've spoken at length with your neighbors. You're a good mother, Joan. You've done a wonderful thing by taking in your sister's daughters. You've given them everything you have. So, believe me. I'm not here to take your daughter... or your daughters, away from you. I'm here to help. I believe we both have the same goal in mind."

Joan choked back a sob that had somehow bubbled up in her throat, and then the tears began to fall in streams.

After some time, the two began to talk as Joan opened up about everything, the adoption process, the loss of her sister, Charlie's withdrawal at her sister's leaving for boarding school, the struggle to keep steady employment.

After what must have been hours, Ms. Filmore gathered her papers and notes together and closed them away in her briefcase with a crisp snap.

"Thank you, Joan. I'll need some time to process this information. If Charlie returns or anything changes, please let me know." Ms. Filmore rose from the table, briefcase in hand, and walked the few steps to the door, opening it as Joan followed her. Turning one last time, the service officer offered a business card with her contact information on it. "Here's my card. Contact me at any time, and especially if Charlie returns or is found."

And with that, the woman closed the door, leaving Joan standing alone in the quiet of her apartment as the light from the spent day dimmed outside.

"Where... Where could you be, Charlie? Where oh where could you be?" Then, lifting her coat from a hook on the wall, Joan opened the door again, exiting the small apartment to resume her furtive search.

Chapter 38

"Woodland Flight, I need eyes! Get me eyes in the skies now. We can't keep fighting blind like this. And can anyone do anything about this darkening fog?" Adeline strode purposefully across the back of the makeshift line they had formed just inside the forest line that encircled the Great Stump. This battle had quickly turned to a route as tendrils of darkness moved like smoke among the Woodling host, obscuring everything.

Millicent's forces had attacked in waves, seemingly more interested in pushing Adeline's Woodlings back than in engaging in actual combat. The sorties had worked, however, as the whole of the Woodling host was trapped between Millicent's army and the Great Stump. Only the Flight of the Forest was able to move without opposition, as Millicent's forces did not appear to include any flying creatures. While this offered at least some kind of advantage, Adeline simply didn't have enough time to think about how to exploit the opportunity.

"Fell the trees! Give us a barrier and some more time," Adeline commanded. "Perhaps Salizar will return with reinforcements in time." Even as the command echoed back to her ears, the ground beneath Adeline's feet began to rumble and shake. Adeline's heart skipped a beat as she realized what this meant. "Millicent must have figured out how to use the key." This she spoke more to herself before lifting her voice and shouting yet another command. "We stand here, Woodlings! Just hold the line as long as you can. Help will come!"

"There is no help for you now, Adeline."

The voice seemed to boom and echo from all around. Millicent had arrived. "Stand down, Adeline, resistance is futile and will only lead to unnecessary loss. For I command the Stone Army!" The voice grew even greater at this pronouncement as a rolling roar accompanied by a trumpet of thunder shook the forest. A blast of turf and snow assailed Adeline from her flank as the ground behind the Woodling army was tossed into the air by enormous stone shapes that were bursting to the surface all around the Great Stump. As the lumbering forms of the massive stone golems emerged from the ground around her, Adeline knew their fight to be lost, as the Stone Army had now trapped the Woodling army and Adeline between their imposing forms and Millicent's forces.

"Enough!" Millicent's voice rang with a clap of thunder and a concussive force that sent many of Adeline's forces sprawling to the ground. The power of the command shook the trees and silenced the creatures on both sides of the conflict, effectively ending the battle though it had barely begun.

"Now..." the heron continued in her precise tones, "Now, the ceremony will be completed as was prescribed... where it began. All we need is the human child." The swirling darkness parted like a curtain a few paces away from Adeline as the heron appeared, walking slowly toward her and the Great Stump.

"You cannot do this, Millicent. You know what will happen. You know what happened the last time this was attempted. Don't be a fool." Adeline glared at the heron as she approached with the confidence of an approaching monarch. Millicent's minions had recovered rapidly and were forming a path through which she strolled easily.

"The only fool I see is the one standing before me," Millicent retorted with a cackle. "Ferris? Deal with this one," she commanded off-handedly as dark shapes leapt around Adeline, teeth glinting with acrid snarls.

"Gladly." Head lowered, Ferris the wolf leader slid through the wall of creatures and stalked confidently toward the antelope. "Come, Adeline. The children are hungry today, and we have a Woodling feast to prepare." The wolf sneered as it barked toward its pack to hem the antelope in and force her away from Millicent's path.

"If you harm even one of these Woodlings, Ferris. You will not live to see another dawn." Adeline's voice was low and fierce, causing the pack around her to back away a step before Ferris barked a laugh in reply.

"Your days are done, Adeline. The wolfpack will lead now. Your tired notions will be swept aside, as they should be. We will be the ones to make the rules now." Ferris laughed then as the wolfpack pushed Adeline to the edge of the forest line with growls and snapping jowls.

With a powerful downstroke of her wings, Millicent rose to the top of the Great Stump and strode to its center, lifting her crystal-taloned foot and beginning to carve deep grooves into the wood, pausing only momentarily to add, "Now, find the girl, and bring her to me."

At her command, Ferris and a group of wolves broke away into the darkness at a run, raising their voices in blood-curdling howls as the rest of Millicent's forces forced the Woodlings to their knees.

Chapter 39

"Well, gentlemen." The voice of Mr. Kettle filled the room as he addressed the small team that sat around the table before him, Brian and Jonathan among them. "It brings me no pleasure to let you know that I've had a fair offer proposed for this building and several other properties that I own." His voice indicated quite the opposite—that he was enjoying telling them precisely this news.

Brian and Jinx stood among the small cohort of other building managers and maintenance chiefs who had been called to the hastily scheduled meeting that morning. They watched from their seats around the crowded conference table as Kettle slowly made his way about the room, finally perching a leg on top of an empty chair that rested against the far wall near a window where the large man considered the view outside as if he were having to make a difficult decision.

"Jinx..." Kettle intoned without looking back to the building manager. "Do you have the paperwork I asked you to draw up?" Kettle didn't bother to look back at Jinx January, who stood quickly from his seat, clutching a folder of papers in his left hand.

"Yes, sir. All of the numbers are here. I've checked them over, and I'm certain they are accurate and up to date." Jinx's response held a note of uncertainty. Heading into the meeting, he had been full of malicious pride at the news he alone held regarding Mr. Kettle's decision about the sale. But Jinx had worked for the man long enough to be cautious when this tone was taken.

"Thank you, Jinx. I'm sure your work is... adequate." Kettle pushed himself back from the window and strode purposefully over to Jinx who offered the folder of papers while the others watched in silence.

"I've decided not to sell." Kettle's words hung in the wood paneled room as shocked expressions appeared en masse among the gathered throng. Even Jinx was shocked at this revelation, as it was not at all what he had been expecting. "You see, when you've been in this business for as long as I, you learn to say 'no' even more than you say 'yes.'" Kettle snatched the folder from Jinx's hand and tossed it carelessly on the center of the table. "But the review of our operations has provided me with excellent insight. You see, by having leadership at each of the buildings, we're literally throwing money away. In fact, I'm quite certain that we could run this operation with a third of the staff we currently have." Mr. Kettle reveled in the sight of so many grown men and women wriggling in their seats.

Brian felt the heat rise to his throat, causing him to unbutton his collar, which Kettle noticed immediately, his dark eyes flashing like a hawk at the first sign of flushed prey.

"Brian, I want you to take the next forty-eight hours to bring me a list of the cuts you can make... and what you would recommend for a leaner more centralized maintenance operation. Do you think you can handle that?" Kettle's eyes twinkled darkly as he watched the red creep further up onto the hot-headed maintenance chief's face.

"It isn't possible, sir. We're short staffed as it is." Brian's face flashed a look of shock, as if he could barely believe he had just uttered those words until they were already out of his mouth.

"Oh? You think we should bring on more people?" Kettle queried with a look of innocent questioning on his face. "Does anyone agree with Brian?" Kettle's sharp gaze cut across the room. No one dared to move. "Come now. Is Brian the only one man enough to disagree with me? You all count yourselves as leaders, and yet you haven't the guts to tell me what you really think?" Kettle's voice was rising now. He was on the hunt. "Fair enough, Brian. You have forty-eight hours to deliver a suitable replacement plan to me." His tone softened for a moment as he walked over to Brian and placed a hand on his shoulder. "And if your plan is no good, you will be the first one I cut." Kettle laughed then, a deep laugh that reverberated in the room as he clapped his hand roughly on Brian's broad shoulder. "Oh, I crack myself up sometimes. You should see your face, Brian." Kettle's laughter slowly subsided into chuckles. "You can present your report to me in forty-eight hours all the same. And, Jinx, do the same for the building managers. I will have both of you back here to present your... well-researched opinions in two days. And if your answers are insufficient, well, let's hope for the both of you that they are not." Kettle chuckled again as he stalked back to his perch near the window. Lifting a leg to rest on the chair, he peered out the window before continuing.

"Now then. Buildings ten and eleven, give me your status updates. I need to be amused."

Chapter 40

The howling of wolves had continued to grow closer throughout the day as the party discussed their options while huddling just outside the circle of stones. As the shadows grew long and the howls grew louder, the planning grew more frantic and the ideas less substantive.

"Well, Charlie Company, I do not believe we can run, therefore, I suggest we prepare to defend ourselves. It is beyond doubt that those wolves are coming for us. All of you should move inside the stone circle, for a single opening is far easier to defend than remaining out here in the open." The Stone Lieutenant had easily taken command of the ragtag group and ordered the construction of a small wall at the lone gap between the standing stones. Yet, no one seemed eager to move into the shadowy confines of the towering structure.

Charlie had participated in gathering stones for the wall and now clutched the remainder of her necklace as she stared into the stone ring, each giant obelisk looking like the tooth of some giant's gaping mouth. The small picture of her sister that she kept inside the locket had burned away, leaving Charlie with an even emptier feeling than she'd had when she first arrived. "I don't like the look of that place," she murmured, not realizing that she had spoken the words aloud.

"Dooooon't like... Don't like!" repeated Mift, now toying with a new phrase to add to his growing collection of human speech. The chipmunk had not been able to help in building the stone wall and had instead ventured up the path of broken ground to search for any sort of clue that might be useful. Having found nothing, she had returned to Charlie's side, watching her every move carefully.

"You know, Mift, I could teach you some proper phrases," Charlie noted absently as she gazed into the yawning mouth of the stone structure. It was just a group of standing stones. Charlie had no idea why the mere sight of them tickled the skin on the back of her neck.

"We haven't time for niceties, Charlie Company. If we're to last until reinforcements arrive, we must be prepared. Now, off you go... get inside while Salizar and your bat friend fly reconnaissance for us, and hopefully find a way to get help from the Woodlings." The lieutenant gazed at Jeremy and Salizar until both of them lifted off the ground and into the air. Salizar dipped and twirled about as the much larger Jeremy flapped mightily until his dark shape disappeared into the dimly lit sky above the dark forest line.

"That leaves Sergeant Pete and I to defend the opening and you and the chipmunk to... stay out of the way." The lieutenant's orders were delivered in matter-of-fact tones.

"Dooooonnnn't like... Don't like!" snipped Mift, who looked comically offended by the insinuation that she would not be useful in defense. Charlie too put her hands to hips and stared at the lieutenant for a moment before offering an open hand to Mift, who reluctantly clambered up Charlie's leg and down her arm, allowing herself to be carried into the dark structure.

"Now, don't you worry, younglings. The Lieutenant and I have seen our fair share of battle, and there's not a wolf alive that scares me," asserted Old Pete bravely, his words punctuated by the odd barking sound of his call and a ruffling of his feathers.

Charlie noted that Old Pete and the lieutenant nearly filled the gap between the stones but wasn't sure that they would be enough to keep the approaching wolves at bay. Nevertheless, cupping Mift in her palm, she stepped across the threshold and into the circle's gloom. As she entered the strange circle of stones, an odd feeling lifted the hairs on her arms and along the back of her neck. It was as if this place were alive. Adding to the strange feeling was the ominous look of the markings etched on the inner side of each of the monoliths. Absently, Charlie noted that the shapes felt familiar and yet completely foreign at the same time.

As Charlie's eyes adjusted to the darkness within the shadow of the stones, she caught sight of the large circular centerpiece that rested heavily in the middle of the structure. Markings covered the large granite slab, which had cracked in half as if struck by a great blow. Taking a step closer to the ruined altar, Charlie's foot crunched, drawing her gaze to her feet where she knelt for closer inspection. Her eyes narrowed as she noticed the tiny white fragments that littered the ground all around her. Reaching out her free hand, she scooped a handful of the strange fragments and gasped as she realized what they were. The bones of many small creatures.

Dropping the handful of bones with a muffled shriek, Charlie quickly stood back to her feet, her eyes catching sight of the carving on the obelisk nearest her, it was the unmistakable image of a coiled snake. As she looked at it, a rattling filled her head. "I don't like this place at all, Mift... not at all."

"Dooooonnnn't like... Don't liiiiike," the small chipmunk replied as it clambered from her hand, up her arm, and onto her shoulder.

As Charlie made her way around the interior of the space, she inspected each etched shape in turn until at last she arrived before the shape of a star circling a moon. The image was mesmerizing. She watched in fascination as the etched lines began to glow with a faint blue hue. Her head felt dizzy, but she couldn't take her eyes away from the glowing shapes which stretched before her in three dimensions as though she were standing on the precipice of a cliff and staring off into the vastness of space.

Mift could feel the energy as well, climbing from Charlie's hand to her shoulder as the little girl walked about the interior of the Place of Stones. Mift had been warned more than once by Adeline not to go near this place, but she could not let the little girl venture in alone. For some reason, the outworlder child was staring deeply at one of the shapes and had grown very still, far too still for a child this young. "Just wake up... just wake up?" Mift chirped in her ear. But Charlie kept staring vacantly ahead. Then the girl began to turn slowly toward the center of the structure, taking one small step at a time toward the large broken altar at the center.

Mift held tightly to Charlie's shoulder as the little girl clambered up onto one sloping half of the slightly angled stone until she was balanced precariously with one foot on either half before turning her gaze back to the monolith that had last drawn her attention. Mift's eyes grew wide as thick smoky tendrils snaked out from not one, but all of the surrounding monoliths, their sinuous lines making their way toward the little girl.

Mift scrambled about from one shoulder to the next, furtively looking up at Charlie and even once nipping her earlobe, but the little girl gave no reaction as the darkness swirled around her feet in a gentle caress. "Just wake up!" Mift chirped the phrase urgently, leaning toward the opening in the doorway to call the others. "Just wake up! Just wake up!" But her tiny voice was drowned out by the thunderous din of the wolf pack who had just arrived.

~❧~

Outside the opening, Old Pete and the Stone Lieutenant stood shoulder to shoulder, guarding the entrance of the stone ring and Charlie as golden eyes appeared at all angles, as if materializing from the shadows of the woods themselves.

"Time is up."

Old Pete knew this voice all too well, and he glowered as Ferris, the wolfpack commander, stepped from the darkness to their right. "Give up the girl, and I promise we'll make this as... painless as possible." Ferris sneered at them, his teeth glinting as he lowered his head and eyed them with a menacing growl.

"Bah. There aren't nearly enough of you to take even me," uttered Old Pete as he puffed his feathers and lowered his head, swaying back and forth as if ready to strike at any moment.

"You are breaking the treaty, traitor." The Lieutenant's head now bore the semblance of a slotted helmet, and a pile of stones near its base quavered with energy and a life of their own.

Ferris let out a laugh followed by a hissing growl. "If it's a fight you want... then a fight you'll have," and even as he was finishing the words, the wolf and a dozen more leapt as one.

Pete dodged and countered with lightning quickness that belied his older age. As he danced in the twilight, the ancient kakapo felt the ferocious hero he once was. He parried flashing jaws with the stroke of a wing, and pounded a head back with his hardened beak, clawing away another with a powerful kick. "Hah ha!" he cried in delight as the memories of battle long forgotten surged back into his thick frame, powering every dip and dive.

Pete noted in his periphery that the Stone Lieutenant was a whirlwind of stone and dust, shattering the gaping mouth of one wolf with a fearsome blow and sending a blast of small round stones that scattered several more. But, years of battle experience told Pete that the two of them could not hold on like this. Not alone. In the height of their youth, it was clear they would have been a force to be reckoned with, but age had taken its toll, and with superior numbers, the wolves would wear down their defense and sap their strength.

To Pete's great relief, Ferris' pack bounded back in retreat after the first slashing attack had been rebuffed by the pair of whirling warriors. Instinct and skill had prevailed against numbers in this first round, but Pete knew the battle to be far from over. As the wolves retreated, Old Pete dropped to the ground, stinging from a dozen small gashes and breathing heavily. "Well, my friend, this might be Old Pete's last stand. Be sure to write a good song for me." Old Pete barked loudly once more and smiled wearily, placing a large wing around the stone lieutenant who too appeared to be flagging.

"Don't give up yet, sergeant. We shall fight to the last of us. Why, look. They have nearly surrounded us. The enemy is to our left and right and straight ahead... we have them exactly where we want them. All we need do is strike in any direction and we shall hit our mark." This the Stone Lieutenant noted in all seriousness, though there might have been a twinkling within eyes of that slotted helmet.

With another chorus of howls, the wolf pack rushed back toward them, causing both Pete and the Stone Lieutenant to give ground. Though they fought bravely, the sheer numbers and ferocity of the wolfpack pushed the pair ever closer to the entrance, unaware of what was happening within.

Ferris, waiting for the ideal moment, leaped and caught Pete on the blind side, staggering the old kakapo as he pounced on top of him, baring his sharpened teeth. "You are finished now…" he growled in savage fury.

Fulcrum

Chapter 41

The scene was one of chaos. Adeline felt the attention of the pack of wolves that were guarding her shift to the power emanating from the heron who stood motionless in the center of the stump. Waves of nauseating darkness pulsed from Millicent as she lifted her wings within the maelstrom of green tinged smoke that twirled about her form like licking flames.

A chorus of cackles and howls filled the night air as Millicent's denizens circled and danced about the Great Stump in a devilish cacophony.

"All of this… such a shame. Fortunately, none of you have the slightest idea what you are doing." No one paid Adeline any notice as her voice was drowned out by the absurd scene that unfolded before her. With a furtive glance, Adeline cast her eyes to her captors, gauging their attentiveness. All were focused intently on Millicent's fiery form. Unbeknownst to most, the Great Stump held a final secret—the tree was still very much alive. Indeed, the roots bore the life of the tree, and while the massive tree had been sheared to within a few feet of the ground, its roots remained intact—roots that delved deep into the ground and stretched throughout the whole of the forest.

Cautiously, Adeline began to edge toward one of the exposed roots. "If I can make it there... perhaps... perhaps I can reach her... perhaps Millicent will listen." She hoped, beyond hope that she was right.

Adeline had been bound tightly with vine, against which she strained. Each moment of painstaking movement drew the vine more tightly against her lithe frame. Yet she need only make the smallest contact with the tree, and so Adeline pressed against her restraints. Finally, trembling from the exertion, Adeline's hoof made contact with the root. Mustering everything she could, the antelope pushed the pain from her bonds to a far corner of her mind and opened her thoughts to connect to the small spark of life that remained in the tree.

Blistering pain accompanied blinding light as Adeline groaned and sagged with the weight of the pain, loss, and sorrow that hit her, staggering her with a thousand memories from cycles upon cycles. And there, within the swirl of sorrow, she sensed a familiar presence. Into this, she poured a very specific memory from their shared youth.

The chaos dissipated in a blink, and Adeline found herself standing at the edge of a large crystalline lake, it's mirror-like surface reflecting a perfectly blue sky. She was taken by the beauty of the scene that spread before her, one of rolling hills and verdant forest. It was the world as it had once been, before everything had changed.

"Bringing me here is a mistake, sister. It will change nothing." The voice belonged to Millicent, who stood a few paces away from Adeline along the lake's edge. "The deed is done, sister. You chose your path and I mine." The Millicent who stood before her now was younger, her colorful plumage deeper, her eyes bright. This was the

Millicent she had grown up with and loved. They'd been inseparable from the moment they had met. Millicent's sharp wit and incisive vision was well balanced by Adeline's steady nature and love for study. They shared a rare grace and had formed a powerful pair that over time came to mold the various factions of creatures into the Woodling society. But Millicent had always been the more ambitious of the two, never satisfied, forever longing for something more.

"I always hoped that things would have turned out differently," commented Adeline as she gazed over the memory's landscape.

"Yet, you knew better, didn't you. I could never convince you of what I saw, but you were attracted to it. It's a shame that you could not shed the old ways and embrace the change that must come." Millicent's form walked further toward the water's edge, peering down at the reflection on the mirrored surface. "But I was a dreamer then too. I thought you and I would lead side by side."

"The blight changed that. And the war. The arrival of the children of Maridil and the promise of power they represent has changed us all." Adeline watched the heron whose head turned slowly back toward her.

"You think?" cackled the heron, ever to the point. "Change is the same as evil in your mind, Adeline. The great fire saved the forest. The drought created new habitats that were better suited for some. The arrival of these outworlders is no different. It is a fire that we can control. We did not invite them, but if we do nothing, our destruction is assured, and that of all of Eridul. We cannot hide away in our Forest and pretend they do not exist. The old ways were always meant to give way to the new. You know this to be true." The heron shook her head slowly.

"The old ways are not old, that is merely your term for them, Millicent." Adeline took a step toward the heron, noticing a slight flickering around the form of the other. "And, yes, change is necessary. I understand that well enough, and I also understand the difference between change and evil. What you are intending to do to the outworld... what you are doing now with this child, this is not change, Millicent. This is chaos, it is the end of all of us. These powers that you hope to wield have their root in Azilem. They are not neutral. You must know this... you MUST feel this."

"You silly child, when will you understand that the source of power is always irrelevant. Whether you harness the sun, or the stars, or the bridge to the outworlds... or the ancient powers. It makes no difference." Millicent punctuated this last phrase as her foot lifted a pebble and tossed it into the pristine water of the memory lake, at once sending ripples in ever widening circles.

"The source makes all the difference, sister. All power seeks its own end. These ancient powers you grasp for now... they are birthed only from the depths of darkness and death. By using them to accomplish your goal, you provide them the path they seek to achieve their own end." Adeline took another step, furrowing her brow as the form of Millicent before her shimmered once again. "It is not too late for us, Millicent. We can lay down our arms, lay down our claims. We can figure this out... together. The girl is the bridge between worlds that we have sought. I admit this. But she can be a beacon of hope and peace. I believe this."

"You cannot delay me any longer, sister. I'm truly sorry. You know that I love you dearly, but my path is chosen, and I must do what must be done. In the end, you will see that I am right. And I will forgive you." A green hued flame flickered at the feet of the heron, her dream-like form slowly being consumed by a thickening darkness. "But for now, Adeline... you must get out of my way!"

The world snapped back in an instant, and with it, pain, as Adeline staggered to her knees. Darkness nearly took her then, but she fought through it. If Millicent would not listen, perhaps she could reach the girl instead. With a force of will, Adeline pushed herself back up, and pressed her hoof once again to the root of the Great Stump.

Chapter 42

"What do you want, Brian? Come to jeer me on?" Jinx sat perplexed before the pile of papers that lay in front of him. Suggesting people to dismiss was not the issue, presenting this as a viable plan that would not end in his own firing was the real puzzle to be solved. And having Brian enter the fray after that debacle of a meeting was the last thing the slender man needed right now. "I don't have time to play at the moment. Why don't you come back later."

Brian sat heavily on the only other chair in Jinx's small office and it creaked as he did so, drawing another look from Jinx. "I can't do it, Jinx. And no matter what I think of you... you can't either."

Jinx looked up at him and smirked before lowering his eyes back to the papers before him. "It's simple really. Kettle gave us the hint when he started with buildings ten and eleven. Their numbers are always the worst, you cut them and be done with it. Easy." Yet Jinx's stomach churned even as the words left his mouth. As much as he hated to admit it, Brian's response was too much a reflection of his own feelings on the matter. But this wasn't about emotion, it was about business and, ultimately, about survival.

"It's nearly Christmas, Jinx… I mean… Jonathan. That's Gary and Norm you're talking about. They both have young families. They have no other source of income. This isn't business anymore. It's… it's just evil." At this last, Brian let out a sigh as he rubbed his temple with a worn hand.

"Evil?" Is this some kind of silly story to you, Brian? Evil… really. It's business. People win and lose every day, and that's just life."

"Is it though? Look at us. Capable, grown men. Incapable of even pushing back against some slimy businessman out of fear. You're afraid, Jonathan. And if you don't do the right thing, you'll be afraid for the rest of your life." Brian's voice was soft and earnest. Something about this situation must have him truly rattled.

"And so what? So I'm afraid. Why shouldn't I be? My family is gone. My wife barely speaks to me anymore. I don't have time to make friends. All I have is this job!" Jinx had no idea where this was coming from, but he was speaking freely now, letting out years of pent up rage in a torrent. "And all this job brings me is misery and idiots like you!" Jinx took little satisfaction as Brian winced at this last comment. Brian was starting to make sense, which was almost as disconcerting as the threat Kettle had leveled against them all.

"Yes, but at least you have me. You have something. I don't have anyone, Jonathan. I don't even have a goldfish. But I will not…" Brian paused to take a breath as he appeared to struggle to hold his rising emotions down. When he resumed, his voice was far calmer. "I will not do this to good people days before Christmas. In fact. I won't do this to good people at all."

"Then you, Brian, are more a fool than I suspected." Jinx's voice was forced and lacked conviction, but at the moment, he just couldn't see another way. And he would not let his guard down any further.

"Then come be a fool with me." Brian rose smoothly from his chair before continuing. "If we all stand together… all of the managers... we can win. I've already talked to the other maintenance chiefs. They are all on board. All we need is a leader, Jonathan." At this, he turned and headed to the door, pausing for a moment in the opening to add, "That could be you."

Chapter 43

"Charlie... Charlie." The thin, precise voice jogged something in the back of Charlie's mind, but Charlie was finding it difficult to focus on where she was, on what she was doing. The memory of recent events seemed to evade her focus as she drifted within a dark fog of twirling tendrils and swirling half tones.

All she wanted to do was rest, to drift away into this dark embrace. Here, she had no cares, no needs, no wants. There was only a faint existence nestled within a soft numb shell.

But the voice was persistent, "Charlie. It's time, Charlie. Time for you to hand the burden to me."

Charlie could not recall hearing this voice before. It reminded her of one of her teachers at school scolding her after being caught daydreaming.

"Come now, Charlie. You only need to reach out to me. Can you do that?" Again, the voice interrupted, cutting through the numbing stupor. This time it seemed as if something gave way above Charlie. For the briefest instant, she thought she heard roars and barks and the howling of wolves, but it was as if those sounds were from some far-off place.

"I… who are you?" Charlie asked at last. "I'm so tired. Do you mind if I rest a bit longer?" Charlie allowed herself to settle back into the caressing tendrils of darkness, and as she did, the opening above her closed once more.

"No, Charlie. It is not alright. You are not finished here. Can't you hear that your friends are in trouble? Wouldn't you like to help them?" The voice was pinprick precise, a sharp and jabbing needle in her head that would not go away.

"Your family needs you too Charlie." Charlie's vision cleared. A vast urban landscape spread below her as though she were looking out at the city from her small bedroom window. Charlie remembered now, she was just asleep in her bedroom, having a very strange, lucid dream. She had no friends, there was no trouble, she just needed to wake up, or go back to sleep without the dream.

"Go away. I want to rest," Charlie responded as she dispelled the vision and settled her mind back into the twirling tendrils of darkness that snaked all about her.

"Well… this will. Not. Do!" snipped the voice, and this time the sky above Charlie parted abruptly as an even darker mote of smoke slammed into her and all around. It was like a torrent of rushing fog, but dry and with a force that curled Charlie's chin down and into her chest, crumpling her until she folded herself into a small ball of arms wrapped around legs.

Charlie shuddered as the fog embraced her, filling her mind and her thoughts with visions of her past. This was all so confusing, a swirl of faces that seemed to float out of her and mingle within the darkness before dissipating as if they had never existed at all.

"Nonie? Cassie?" "Mama!" Familiar faces drifted off, and with them, their memory seemed to fade as well. "I don't… what is happening? What… what are you doing? I want it to stop… please make it stop!" With each passing moment, Charlie felt more weary than the last.

"Only a moment more, child, and then... then I will be finished with you, and your purpose here will be... complete," the strange voice hissed.

Chapter 44

Salizar fluttered in futile bursts, attempting to keep pace with Jeremy's soaring form. For all his clumsiness on the ground, the dark bat was a marvel to behold in the air, beating his enormous leathery wings in broad air gulping sweeps. The scene below them was one of colossal destruction. A jumbled path had been torn through the forest canopy in the shape of a three toothed wedge. Details of what was within that wedge were unfortunately obscured by a seething cloud of darkness. Even at this great height, Salizar could sense the felling of each tree as the massive host rolled onward to the north, destroying the forest as they went.

A sudden shadow overhead sent the small finch into an immediate dive, but it was too late as a powerful claw clapped itself around his entire body, leaving Salizar trapped below the punishing strokes of a much larger bird's wings. After a brief and fruitless struggle, Salizar relaxed, consigned to his imminent doom.

"Fear not, little one. I would not have caught you if I meant to harm you. You, your friend, and I need to have a little chat is all." The voice from above was oddly familiar. So familiar in fact that Salizar froze in panic. It was the same voice that he had heard speaking from the shadows on the day that Charlie had been taken.

"You'll not get away with this," Salizar chirped, trying to make his voice sound as calm as possible given the circumstances. "My friends will not take kindly to you treating me like this."

"Calm down, friend. Didn't you hear what I just said? I'm here to talk to you and the bat... who, by the way, is an outworlder just like me." With a few more powerful strokes, the kea advanced on the large bat, drawing nearly even with Jeremy's outstretched wings. "Isn't that right, Jeremy? We go way back, don't we?"

This comment drew the bat's attention, his flight faltering momentarily in evident surprise. "That voice is familiar." Apparently, Jeremy's echolocation was not finely tuned enough to recognize Salizar being held captive in Kraftin's grip.

"Follow me below, old friend. I have information that you need to hear. You're too late to stop this army, but you're not too late to help your new friends." Kraftin wheeled away from the bat, diving rapidly toward a small patch of open turf on the ground far below. The speed was such that poor Salizar nearly blacked out, but the flight was over in a rush as the kea's powerful wings drew them up short of the ground in a graceful and expert landing, though the kea retained his tight grip on Salizar.

Jeremy's descent took much longer as he glided in circles, drawing closer with each pass until he landed with a thump near the edge of the clearing. Cautiously, the larger fruit bat approached, making soft clicking noises as he did so. "Ah, I see now that you have my friend," Jeremy glowered, having at last noticed Salizar in the kea's grip.

"I'll let your little friend go free in a moment, but first, you need to let me speak." The kea balanced on one leg while lifting Salizar up in a threatening gesture.

With all of his strength, Salizar bit down on the kea's claw, resulting in a satisfying squawk from the larger bird, who released him immediately.

"Well, now, aren't we a feisty one." Kraftin snarled as Salizar tested his wings while skittering away from the predatory bird.

"You just stay back, you brute. We have an important task to perform, and you are slowing us down." Salizar took to the air quickly and flitted his way over to Jeremy before alighting and beginning to inspect his wings with a probing beak.

A deep and rumbling growl cut through the chatter as Kraftin' tiger companion lumbered into the clearing his white fur taking on a sinister blood red hue under the dull light of the waxing moon above.

"Your friends will be dead soon if you don't... control yourselves and consider our proposal." Marvelous' deep voice rumbled with each carefully placed step, the tiger's head was lowered, and his haunches were poised for a leap. "Not that I care either way."

"What do you know about our friends? What are you talking about?" chirped the finch in reply, his eyes blinking in agitation.

"As we waste time here, the wolf pack is on its way to the stone circle... where your friends are. They are after the girl." The response came again from the enormous tiger, who had not stopped its slow pace toward Jeremy and Salizar.

"We offer our aid, dear friends. And, quite frankly, you are in no position to deny our... assistance." Kraftin's eyes narrowed as he looked first at Marvelous and then back toward the pair.

"We want no help from the two of you," chirped Salizar. He was about to say something further but was interrupted by Jeremy.

"What do you want in exchange, Kraftin?" Jeremy's tone surprised Salizar, who had only ever heard the bat's jovial and meek demeanor. Jeremy sounded more confident, or at least more familiar. Clearly, he knew these two.

"Ah, practical as always, Jeremy. Our deal is simple. We help you save your friends, and you in return, you help us stop that scraggly old bird... isn't that what you intend to do anyway?" Kraftin smiled back at the pair of them.

"We don't have all night. If we are to make it back in time, you must make your choice now." The Marvelous had paused in his approach, head still lowered, watching the small bird and the bat with narrowed eyes and a low rumble building in his chest.

"Salizar, my friend. You may not trust them, but I don't think we have a choice. We need their help." Jeremy had turned toward the finch, his voice sullen and heavy. "It is true that I knew them in what you call the outworld. We... worked together, you might say, and while neither can be trusted, both are... quite talented."

Salizar fidgeted in his perch. Jeremy was right and these two creatures were right, but every instinct told him this was all wrong. Nevertheless, time was indeed short, and so Salizar found himself reluctantly conceding. "I have a terrible feeling about this, but... very well. What is your plan?"

Visibly, the tiger relaxed at Salizar's words, and the four converged for a brief discussion before departing with speed back toward the Place of Stones.

Chapter 45

The wind whipped across the field, whistling past the large white monuments that stood tall amidst the rows upon rows of smaller headstones and grave markers. Remnants of wreaths along with a few weather-beaten mementos resting at the base of a gravestone here and there marked a loved one's visit with a memory.

Joan shivered as she pulled her winter coat more closely around herself, but without trees or buildings, the bitter wind cut through the wool fiber as though she wore nothing at all. She was numb from head to toe but felt none of it. For some time, she had wandered about the cemetery, knowing that her feet would eventually take her to the familiar place she had once visited with far greater regularity.

"Janet Samantha Cole," Joan whispered, her breath emitting as a puff of steam into the air before being swept away by the chill breeze. Her sister had bucked the family tradition by taking her husband's name in its entirety when they wed. "Easier to spell and gave you a better spot on every list." Joan smiled at her sister's explanation. In truth, she hardly blamed Janet, as Cole was a good name, and her husband Charles a better man.

But she wasn't here to reminisce today. Today she needed advice. "Janet. I... I've lost Charlie." The words caught in her throat even as she spoke them. "I don't know where she is... I can't believe she would just run away like this, but... I don't know where else to turn."

Now that the first words were out, Joan felt emboldened to continue. "I think she must have run away, must be hiding somewhere, but it's been more than a day, and she hasn't returned." Joan's voice dropped at the end of the sentence, that familiar mixture of grief and anger welling up from deep within. "I had to let Cassie go to the school. I know it's what you would have done, and it was the right thing. I just... I just wasn't prepared for any of this." Joan pulled her gloved hands from the shallow pockets of her coat. She held a small glass figurine in her palm, and it glistened in the cool winter light.

"You gave this to me the last time we were together. Do you remember?" Joan sighed, knowing full well that she was talking into empty air. Yet, she bent to place the small figure on the rounded top of the headstone, which was a simple piece of white marble, the type of thing the cemetery provided to those who could afford nothing else.

Joan shivered as she straightened. She idly kicked at a tuft of frozen turf with the toe of her boot. "Where did you go, Janet?" The words were out of her mouth before she could think. With a furtive glance, she looked around the empty graveyard, as if worried that someone might hear. Seeing no one, she knelt down toward the small, rounded headstone.

"I've kept my promise, Janet. The girls don't know. No one knows, but... Janet, if you are out there somewhere, you have got to help me." Joan reached out a hand to brush away a fresh smattering of snowflakes that had just landed on top of the headstone.

"I know what the police said, they said you drowned. They said your body was washed away, but, Janet... I can feel you!" Her voice had risen now, even as tears began to freeze at the corners of her eyes. She made a fist with her hand and pounded the top of the headstone as a sob broke the silence. "Janet... Charlie is gone ... I can't lose her too. I can't lose her like I lost you." Joan was now gripping the top of the headstone with both hands, her head bowed between her arms as she fell to her knees and breathed deeply to catch her breath.

"Why did you leave me? Why did you run out into the night like that? It was... it was just a stupid argument. I should never have spoken about Charles like that, but you know me... you know I didn't mean it." Joan's voice drifted off. She remembered the night well. Janet had sworn that Charles had not abandoned them, that he had disappeared and needed help. She'd been hysterical and made no sense. All Joan had tried to do was break through Janet's panic. But the opposite had taken place, ending with Janet fleeing into the night.

Joan's tears dripped to the snowy ground as the wind whistled across the cemetery. Each drop melting the snow as they landed, and then freezing as they were caressed by the ceaseless blustering wind. Releasing her grip on the headstone and dropping her hands to her knees, Joan pushed herself up, taking another deep breath to steady her breathing. Brushing snow from her knees, Joan turned silently away. Nothing she said now could change what had happened. The only thing that mattered now was Charlie, and Joan needed to focus her energy on finding her daughter as soon as possible.

The small figurine glistened in the fading light as the wind continued to blow across the now empty cemetery. Each wintry breath buffeted the fragile object closer to the edge of the headstone until one last swirling gust sent it tumbling to the ground where it clicked as it bounced off of the frozen turf to land within the small circle shaped by Joan's tears. As the chill winter light glinted from its crystalline surface, snowflakes began to cover the tiny glass figurine of a moon and a star.

Sacrifice

Chapter 46

Ferris smiled viciously, rearing his head back and opening his teeth-lined jaws for a killing strike when the ground abruptly gave way beneath the wolf pack leader. Strong wings beat on either side as the scene of the battle grew smaller and smaller until only the tops of the trees of the forest could be seen. The wolf squirmed frantically against his assailants to no avail as he was lifted higher and higher into the twilight sky.

And then, a release, followed by the rush of oncoming air as two shadowy winged creatures swooped away, leaving Ferris tumbling back toward the earth, a final howling shriek rending the night air.

"A good plan, my new friend." The voice of Jeremy could only just be heard as he tucked his wings and plummeted in tandem with Kraftin, his tenuous new ally. Together, the large bat and parrot-like bird-of-prey targeted another wolf—dove, snagged, lifted, and dropped. Again and again with ruthless efficiency, the two worked to clear the field.

With the weight of Ferris suddenly gone, Old Pete staggered back to his feet just in time to shudder at the thunderous roar of a tiger, whose massive, muscled form leaped from the darkness to land next to him, teeth snapping at the nearest wolf.

"Fear not, bird. Reinforcements have arrived," growled Marvelous as his white frame glinted in the twilight and seemed to blend eerily with the shadow speckled snow. Immediately, Marvelous pounced away as one, two, three, and more wolf-like forms were sent sprawling.

"Ah. About time we received reinforcements, and a worthy compatriot," noted the Stone Lieutenant as she too was able to take a moment's rest from the attack, gathering a stream of stones about her and now rolling forward in the wake of the tiger's attack, pushing the pack back. But now, the wolves were disappearing rapidly, somehow being lifted straight into the dark night sky, to be followed by a long howling shriek. And then a familiar twittering sound caught Pete's attention, heralding the finch's return.

"Oh my... oh my... I hope this was the right thing to do..." Salizar alighted on the head of the Stone Lieutenant as the remainder of the wolf pack began to turn and retreat back into the darkness of the tall trees.

Apparently unable to counter the might of the great tiger, and having taken notice at last of the aerial attack, the remaining wolves fled, first one at a time and then all were fleeing back into the shadows from whence they had come.

As swiftly as the battle had begun, silence returned, and with it, two large, winged creatures landed abruptly before the Stone Lieutenant as the muscled tiger padded back from the edge of the forest. Seeing the group converging, Old Pete fluffed his feathers and tenderly waddled over with a noticeable limp.

"An exceptional counter, I must say. Very fine work, troops, very fine indeed." The face of the stone lieutenant slid back to that of eyes and nose with a grinding crunch, its war-like helmet no longer visible. "But I have not seen you before, are you outworlders?" the lieutenant queried, eyeing Kraftin and Marvelous with an appraising gaze.

"I apologize for not having introduced ourselves earlier, but it seemed wiser to take action first."

Old Pete followed the assured form of the kea as it stepped into a waning beam of light, its magnificent green feathers shimmering metallically as it cocked its head in assessment of the small group that now stood in a makeshift circle just beyond the opening of the circle of stones.

"Allow me to introduce myself," the parrot-like bird replied. "My name is Kraftin. This magnificent creature... is Marvelous. And we are indeed as you call us... outworlders." Having swept a wing toward the tiger in introduction, Kraftin tipped his beak without breaking eye contact with the lieutenant. "It was a good thing that Marvelous and I happened to find Jeremy here," the kea noted with a grin. "A surprising but familiar face in this strange place, as he too is one of our kind ... an outworlder, as you say." Kraftin tilted his head back toward the large fruit bat who had remained outside the rough circle created by the converging creatures. Pete felt himself tensing as he watched the strange bird. This one was not to be trusted.

"Oh, yes... yes, we have performed together before in the other... world, as you call it," confirmed Jeremy before being cut off by Kraftin.

"As for me, I do not believe in coincidence. You see, I and my compatriot Marvelous here were sent from our own world to yours to ensure the safety of a small human child... but we have not been able to find her, I'm afraid."

"Well, then it is indeed fortunate that you have arrived. For we…" The Stone Lieutenant was in turn cut-off by a flurry of wings above its head and the chirping voice of Salizar.

"Oh yes, very, very fortunate indeed… if only we had seen a human… why, it has been… many cycles since I or my friends here have…" Salizar was himself interrupted by the loud sniff of the formidable white tiger.

"Hmmmmm… you smell… familiar… don't you have a little friend as well?" Marvelous' deep voice rolled from his chest as he leaned toward the dipping movements of the small finch. Old Pete shuffled a step or two more closely to Salizar. He was certain now that something was exceedingly wrong about these two newcomers. He only wished his mind would speed up a bit and figure out what it was that he felt was missing.

"I think we're all just a bit frazzled from the fight… eh?" interjected Kraftin smoothly. "Say, I was just here not long ago… right before that crazy heron started to raise a ruckus. I believe I may have dropped something inside that circle of stones. Do you mind if I take a look around?" Kraftin was already heading in the direction of the looming stones as the others watched curiously. But Pete and Salizar must have shared the same instinct as Salizar fluttered quickly ahead of Pete, trying to keep himself between the opening to the circle and the approaching kea. The battle had taken everything out of the old warrior and he was uncertain if he could do anything at all to stop these two from finding Charlie.

Salizar flipped easily past Pete to settle himself on a rock just outside the entrance as Pete puffed up to his side. "Not another step, you!" Salizar trilled. "You were working with Millicent, and while we thank you for saving our friends, there is nothing here of interest for you."

"Oh... I'm quite sure that I'll be the judge of that," hissed Kraftin. Even as the words left the kea's beak, a sharp cry from Mift drifted out from within the stone structure.

"Just wake up! Jusssst wake up!"

Old Pete turned with a start, waddling as quickly as he could with the rest of them toward Mift's insistent call. He came to a shocking halt as he took in the scene unraveling before him. Barely visible as he clung to Charlie's still form was Mift, but he was not the object of Pete's amazement. For there was Charlie, wrapped in darkness and suspended over the center of the broken stone altar as a greasy smoke poured from everywhere, wrapping her in its sinuous tentacles. More shocking was the thick stream of darkness that lifted from her suspended body to the top of the standing stones before arcing out of the top of the circle of monoliths and away toward what could only be the direction of the Great Stump... where Millicent and her forces had gone.

Pete gasped as recognition at last bloomed in his aging mind. He had glimpsed this very scene once long ago... with another female soft skin. It was a sacrifice, he knew, a sacrifice to break the barrier between worlds. A rustle to his right pulled the old warrior's attention back to the newest members of the small party. But he could not react in time as he heard the fierce looking bird-like creature hiss, "Marvelous... you know what to do."

At this command, the tiger leapt with gaping mouth and a fierce roar.

Chapter 47

"Charlie... Charlie." This time the voice was different... more familiar. But Charlie in her haze could barely focus long enough to care. She wanted to rest. She needed to rest. But again, the voice was persistent... not like it was before, for this time it sounded both gentle and sad.

"Charlie... This is Adeline. If you can hear me, Charlie, we need your help... we need you to do something that only you can do." Something inside her mind rang like a small bell as the voice spoke. And in spite of the great weariness that lay over her, Charlie roused her mind enough to reply.

"I'm so tired. Please leave me alone... please. Let me go." An image flashed into Charlie's mind of a once proud creature, now bound and broken, being jostled by large howling bodies and scraped with horns and claws. But the image faded as quickly as it had appeared and Charlie settled back into a sleepy haze.

"I can hear you, Charlie. It's me. Adeline. This isn't a dream. You are trapped. But you have the power to free yourself and all of your friends." Charlie's waking mind grudgingly recognized the voice she had heard upon arriving in this strange place. That seemed so long ago. This sounded like the antelope that had met her at the beginning of this journey. But as she recalled, that antelope had left her all alone in the first place.

"I have no friends here. All of you just want something from me. Just... just leave me alone."

"Charlie, I'm sorry." The intrusive voice refused to go away. There was a desperation to it, but a kindness too that made Charlie's heart ache. "This isn't your world. You owe nothing to us. But we are in desperate need. And you are right. The price we ask of you is too high. But if you do nothing, you will lose everything too... your real home and those who have come to love you here."

"No one... no one loves me. Everyone has abandoned me." Charlie desperately wished that what the voice claimed were true. She had felt so alone, so unnecessary and unloved since her sister left. But no, these were the vacant words of another adult. "You're wrong, Adeline. Everyone is wrong. I have nothing to give any of you."

"No, Charlie... but don't take my word for it... look with your own eyes... with your own heart... for where your heart leads, your spirit will follow."

Once again, an image snapped into Charlie's mind of the graceful antelope Adeline shaking herself free of her bonds and gathering what strength remained. Slipping free of the vines and briars that had constrained her, Charlie watched as Adeline leaped to the top of the largest stump she had ever seen, so large that it could only have been a dream. Adeline's hooves slipped on the slick wooden surface as she attempted to find purchase. But as her hooves dug in she turned and dashed into a burning vortex that swirled at the center of a menagerie of cavorting, howling shapes.

As Charlie watched the antelope enter the swirling boundary of fire, sparks burst like fireworks all along the darkling bridge that streamed away from the storm at the center of the snarling horde.

Charlie could feel its effect as the air around her tingled and sparked. A concussive blast shook the imposing stones and rumbled through the ground below, leaving a high pitched tone ringing in her ears.

In that moment, Charlie's eyes cleared. She saw herself suspended in the air as the tiny figure of Mift leapt from her shoulder straight into the gaping jaws of a roaring tiger that was even now flying directly toward her.

And then... everything froze.

Chapter 48

Salizar saw it all unfold, powerless to act. As the tiger leapt, his dearest friend Mift dove straight at Marvelous with a boundless courage that none could match. Salizar saw the girl's eyes open wide in shock and then terror and then... something different. It was not rage, nor sorrow, it was neither hope nor fear, but something in between all of those things.

The look in her eyes froze everything around her as time itself gave way to her will. And there... from the center of her chest, a light began to pulse and gleam. Dimly at first, but then with greater purpose and power. It infected the darkness around her, scattering the inky void like mere motes of dust until the child shone brightly, too brightly to watch. But Salizar could not close his eyes, caught as he was in mid-flight... frozen in time like all the world around him.

And then... a sound. Not a sound of sorrow or pain, not a deep rumble or a screeching hiss, but the sound of some ancient song, one that he had always known but was hearing again as if for the first time. The strains of this song lifted all around the shining form of the small child as she raised her hands into the air and opened them, palms aloft, toward the sky above.

In that instant, Salizar understood. It was not the locket, nor the battle. It was not the dominance that one creature held over another. It was not the child. It was love… not the silly fleeting feelings of which mundane attraction were construed, but the power of one stranger's willingness to sacrifice all that they are for another. It was the love that believed all things, hoped all things… a love that only someone with everything to lose could possibly give. Charlie was not giving in… she was gifting all as only a child could. How could they all have been so callow.

Then light, like that of a thousand suns, poured from the child in undulating, pulsing rivers. Rivers that turned to torrents, rending the darkness that breaths ago had looked an impenetrable barrier. And as the light grew in strength, so did the song, until it burst away from the girl at its center in a rolling, roaring shockwave that knocked Salizar from the sky and sent him twirling and tumbling to the snowy ground below.

There the small finch lay, unable to hear, unable to feel or to see anything but the blinding light and faint ringing in his ears. As the ringing faded he picked himself up from the ground, shaking his feathers and checking his wings. There was Old Pete, he too was stumbling to his feet. The rocks and pebbles that comprised the Stone Lieutenant's body had been blown apart but were now gathering back together into their familiar martial form. Of the tiger and the kea there was no sign. And the little girl too had vanished, along with…

"Mift…"

Chapter 49

M r. Kettle lounged behind the large wooden desk in his formal office. He only invited people into this room when the situation called for something a little extra.

The woman who sat primly on the edge of the low chair in front of the desk appeared to be the typical government type. She was neat as a pin, showing little emotion, with her dark hair pulled back and her gray suit providing no conversational prompts. But she had done what he expected upon entering the room. Her eyes had taken in the sights and trophies of his years of business conquests and political networking. His office was adorned with name dropping photos, gifts, notes, and awards.

"I see you are a person who can appreciate a businessman like myself. Why, the stories this room could tell." He tilted in his seat and reached out to a glass box that held a police shield. "The chief presented this to me last winter I believe…" Kettle mused as if having seen it for the first time and marveling at the circumstances surrounding the gifting of such a thing. "To our very own Gotham knight," read Kettle from the inscription. "The police admire the work I've done in helping to curb illicit activities here in the Flats."

His voice trailed off as he looked over to the woman whose expression remained unchanged.

※

Ms. Filmore sat patiently as she waited for the inevitable bloviation to take its course. The room was impressive, as was the incredible evidence of graft the man had accumulated over his years in control of the Eastern Flats. Rather than listening further to this continuing charade, Ms. Filmore lifted her smooth black briefcase to her lap and clicked the locks open before raising the lid. She withdrew a manilla envelope that concealed the thick document she had carried with her for the meeting today. After setting the briefcase on the ground again, she stood and took a step toward his desk, setting the envelope there and placing her hand on it as she leaned in toward his seated form. Two could play this game.

"Mr. Kettle. I appreciate the unfettered access you granted me in the child abandonment investigation that brought me to your building. And I have prepared a report that I would like to share with you regarding my findings before I take further action with the family involved." Her voice cut through the haze of the room, causing Kettle to roll his cushioned chair away from her as she now towered over his seated position.

"Well that won't be necessary, my dear. Why don't you just leave that with me. I'm sure we both have better things to do." Kettle was stalling now, perhaps confused as he attempted to discern her motivation.

"Oh, I will." Ms. Filmore smiled as she lifted the envelope from the desk and stepped back a pace. But her piercing gaze never left him. "But first, I thought it would only be fair to share my findings... As a professional courtesy, of course." The corners of her mouth compressed slightly. "I see that you have created quite the network in this small part of the city." She emphasized the word small specifically to elicit the reaction she was now seeing on his face as a slight flush grew around the collar of his shirt. "I too have a number of friends who I've been reviewing my case information with, and they suggested that things might not be as rosy as they appear."

"I see." Kettle's countenance twisted as the woman continued. His face was darkening with menace, like the gathering clouds of a brewing storm. "I think I have heard quite enough, Ms. Filmore? Why don't you leave those documents with me. I have a pressing appointment with... the mayor that I wouldn't want to miss."

But Ms. Filmore continued unphased, "So we are dispensing with the niceties then? Fair enough. Mr. Kettle, the State has investigated a suspected issue of child abandonment and neglect with one of the residents of your state and federally subsidized tenant buildings. While that case remains open, in the course of our investigation, and in keeping with established memoranda between our departments, I have shared my findings regarding your compliance with the relevant laws and regulations that may impact our findings."

Mr. Kettle crashed to his feet, knocking his chair backward and into the display case behind him, rattling the contents within. "That's enough, woman. You should leave now before this becomes unpleasant." His meaty hand reached toward the phone on his desk but paused before lifting the receiver.

The one thing that no longer surprised Ms. Filmore was the instinct of a cornered man to threaten violence. And while this particular man appeared more likely than most to actually make good on his threat, she knew now that she had taken the right course of action. With this confirmation in mind, she offered the manilla envelope toward him, having the expected effect of cutting through his rising emotion. "Here, the details are inside."

Mr. Kettle reached over the desk and quickly swiped the folder from her hand, tearing at the small string that held the package closed. "And what is this, exactly." Kettle's voice was a veritable snarl.

Ms. Filmore gave him a moment to open the envelope and begin to slide out the bound document, its embossed seal glinting in the dim light. "You, Mr. Kettle... have been served. Mr. Harvey Kettle, as the proprietor of Kettle Holdings, you are summoned to appear before the District Court to respond to federal and state charges for the violation of multiple regulations and requirements of the Fair Housing Act."

Kettle removed the papers as she spoke. His fingers crumpled the pages as veins began to pulse along his temples. His breathing shallowed as his eyes scanned the pages, and she knew then that she stood on the precipice of imminent danger. Yet, she pressed forward.

"Your residents have the right to live in decent, safe, and sanitary housing that is free from environmental hazards. They have the right to have repairs performed in a timely manner, upon request. They have the right to organize as residents without obstruction, harassment, or retaliation from property owners or management. And, Mr. Kettle, the families who live in these buildings absolutely have the right to be free of your systemic discrimination based on familial status."

Slamming the papers onto the heavy desk, Mr. Kettle did not look up at her, his eyes boring into the deeply stained wood. Perhaps he was held in check by the thin thread of sense that doing anything else here would only weaken his position. Filmore watched with an oddly detached fascination as Kettle breathed heavily before replying.

"Get out..." his voice was a whispered rasp as his eyes continued to bore into the desktop in front of him.

Ms. Gladys Filmore had already retrieved her briefcase, and without a second look, slipped silently out of the office. There was one last task she needed to perform.

Chapter 50

Days passed as the small group of Woodlings gathered at the site of the Great Stump. A wreath of flowers had grown all along its wide base, and in the very center of the cracked wood grew a slender sapling, its thin green needles glistening in the light that poured from the clear blue sky above.

The twilight had given way to the first morning in anyone's remembrance.

Gone were the wolves and wild creatures. They had slunk away after the miracle of the night before. In the climax of the heron's piercing chant, a blinding light had descended on the whole of the stump, obliterating everything in its path and sending the evils of the night tumbling at the front of a mighty wave of power that none could describe. Only those Woodlings who stayed true to the forest remained, though even these had been knocked to the ground by a mighty concussive blow.

Millicent was gone, and in her place stood this beautiful young sapling. All that remained atop the surface of the Great Stump was the small tree and the still, limp form of Adeline.

For many cycles, there would be debate about what exactly happened that night. Each of the Woodlings had witnessed something different, and each had a story to tell more fascinating than the next. Some had seen their ancestors return to strike blows against the prancing creatures of darkness. Others swore that Adeline herself had defeated Millicent in a climactic battle. Still others saw the form of a small glowing child appear and take the heron into an embrace that formed the small tree that now grew at the center.

For Salizar, who had taken up residence in a crook of one of the surrounding trees, all he knew was that his dear sister Mift was gone. And yet, while sorrow filled his heart, he felt certain that this was what was always meant to be.

And so in the days that succeeded that momentous event, Salizar had taken to the task of learning to scribe his and others' memories down on small rolls of bark that he had instructed a handful of Woodlings to store in a small rock enclosure that had been erected next to the Great Stump. It was his hope that the lessons learned and the heroes who stood tall against the darkness might never be forgotten.

"Ah, ah... careful there... that one goes to the right of the big one. But carefully... I'll not have you spoil a single scroll." Salizar shook his tiny head in amusement. He would also need to teach these young Woodlings a thing or two... perhaps build one of those schools that Charlie had mentioned in an off-handed comment during their travels.

Chapter 51

Another day had dawned as bright as the last. The shimmering blue sky was lit by a golden sun that banished the chill from the air. The snow had melted away, and in its place new growth had begun to bloom, with tiny flowers expanding in colorful bursts all around.

"Well, I suppose our work here is done." The Stone Lieutenant stood before her army, surveying the work they had completed at last. The trees that had been uprooted by the Stone Army had been cleaned, shorn, and stored as building material. The torn ground was smoothed back, and with the help of the Woodlings, small saplings had been planted all along the stretch of newly flattened ground. The Place of Stones had been dismantled once and for all. And the stones themselves had been ground into fine gravel and spread over the ground where a single marking stone was erected as a reminder of the sacrifices that had been made.

"You there, sergeant," continued the lieutenant as she pointed a finger toward Old Pete. The large kakapo had decided to take a seat under the shade of a tree. "No one said you could take a break. Up now. We are nearly finished here, all that remains is the final salute, and then we'll be off."

Old Pete pulled himself wearily to his feet, shaking gravel dust from his feathers. "Well, these old bones have had all the adventure they need for quite some time." The old flightless bird looked about and then sighed. "I sure do miss the little fellow... mighty brave thing she did... mighty foolish but mighty brave all the same."

"Alright then. Company! Atttennnntion!" The Stone Lieutenant's voice rang out loud and clear as the sun crested overhead. The Woodlings that had gathered to commemorate the moment, drew themselves into a half circle several paces from where the lieutenant stood atop a makeshift platform. The giant shapes of several remaining members of the Stone Army, huge golem-like creatures, thumped to the rear of the assembly. Finally, all drew silent as the Stone Lieutenant began to address them.

"We gather this day in honor of our fallen friends.

To commemorate their deeds and to consecrate these hallowed grounds.

Let it be known this day that a great battle was lost, not won.

For of all our might, and all our training,

It was not the mighty among us who saved the day,

But the smallest and brightest.

Today we honor those who have gone before us.

Let their deeds remain forever in our hearts.

Let their courage be our guiding star should darkness ever return

And let the light of their memory always illuminate the path before us.

Our friends, our compatriots, we salute you!"

At this, the members of the Stone Army clapped their massive boulders together, and blew somber tones on their immense horns of war, marking the moment in thunderous notes that echoed across the valley, through the trees and up into the vibrant blue sky above.

Very Bright

Chapter 52

"Look at this nonsense," spewed Mr. Kettle, spittle flying from his lips as he tossed a folder filled with loose papers toward the shaken form of Jinx, who he had called into his office in an attempt to deal with the disaster that had unfolded at the hands of the petit case officer.

Jinx looked on as Kettle prowled about his office like a caged tiger. The man looked positively unhinged, more so than Jinx had ever seen. Jinx was burning with desire to pick the folder up but dared not move while the volatile man was in this kind of rage.

"No one does this to me," Kettle seethed, pounding his fists into his heavy wooden desk before turning his maniacal gaze toward Jinx. "You need to make this go away, Jinx. Do whatever you need to do. But this... this insanity..." Kettle grabbed a heavy square paperweight and without a second thought sent it sailing into the wall to his left. Framed pictures and plaques fell in a crash to the floor as the points of the marble paperweight jutted from the wall in their place.

"Go ahead! Pick it up, Jinx. I can see that you're dying to look at it!" In a blink, Kettle had taken quick strides to reach the much smaller Jinx, grabbing the folder in his hand as papers scattered to the floor and pressing it heavily to Jinx's chest as he leaned in. "I know you, Jinx... I made you who you are, I can smell the fear on you. But even that pales in comparison to the stench of greed that rolls off you."

Jinx could feel Kettle's hot breath on his face, the man's fetid odor making his eyes water. But instinctively, he cupped the stack of papers with an arm, taking a step back.

Mr. Kettle didn't appear to notice as he had already turned his back to Jinx and was now eyeing the varying ornaments that remained on his desk as if looking for another object to hurl.

Scanning the papers quickly, Jinx could tell immediately that this was a court summons and notice of a lawsuit. But the federal seal mingled with a state seal told Jinx everything he needed to know. This was something very different than a mere resident complaint or a standard audit. Hastily, he lifted the messenger bag he had carried into the office with him and shoved the papers inside, moving swiftly about the room to collect the sheets that had fallen to the floor. As he stood back up, Kettle was eyeing him, holding a weighty metal bust in his right hand and grinning in a vile manner.

When Kettle spoke again, his voice was low, befitting the haunted and crazed look in his eyes. "We're going to make them pay, Jinx. You and I. Together, we're going to take them down. All of them. And we begin today. Everyone in the building who hasn't paid rent must now pay double." Kettle held the base of the heavy metal bust in his hand and slammed it into the wooden desk, making a dent in the hard wood surface with a deep booming sound that caused Jinx to jump.

Yet Kettle continued. "Anyone who is currently late on rent. Double what they owe." Another pounding of metal to wood followed by a deep chuckle. Clearly, Kettle had lost it completely.

And then something inside Jinx snapped. Just as Kettle was about to make another pronouncement, Jinx silenced him with a single word.

"No."

Kettle was so shocked, he blinked before replying, "No, Harvey." Jinx had never before used his boss's first name, and the effect was plain as Kettle now took a step back, looking like some great and unforeseen foe had entered the room. "That isn't what we're going to do." Jinx couldn't believe what he was saying but felt as though there were no turning back now. "But I'll tell you what I'm going to do." Jinx patted the satchel that now contained the summons.

"And what... exactly is the pathetic... scrawny... insignificant weasel that you are... going to do?" Kettle's voice seethed as he took a step toward Jinx, who had already retreated to the door and placed a hand on the latch.

"I'm going to cooperate fully. Merry Christmas, Mr. Kettle. Merry Christmas." Jinx flung the door wide and jumped out just as the metal bust sailed past his ear into the wall behind the door. But Jinx kept moving as Kettle's howls followed him through the hallway and out into the snow.

Chapter 53

Not knowing what else to do, Brian had gone back to the basics—fixing things. Having left Jinx, he had let his feet carry him back to his own office where he picked up the familiar tool pouch, returned to the bank of elevators, and hit the button for the forty-third floor.

The elevator hummed around him but didn't stop until it reached its destination, as he had used his express key to take the uninterrupted route to the floor. Stepping out into the hallway, he walked slowly to apartment forty-three twelve and pressed the room bell. Nothing. This time, Brian knocked gently on the door, but rather than the door to forty-three twelve opening, the door across the hall did as an elderly woman with long graying hair wrapped in a braided bun looked tentatively out into the hall.

"Um. Excuse me, ma'am, I'm Brian, with maintenance. I was told to drop by this unit to check the ventilation, but no one seems to be home." Brian had permission to enter Joan's apartment, but knew from prior experience that it was best to inquire around and make his actions known rather than having strange rumors build. Besides, while this was a safe floor, the practice had saved him on numerous occasions in some of the more dangerous parts of the building. One never knew exactly what they might find behind a closed door.

"Yes, yes, I know who you are and... Well, Joan is not in at the moment." Ms. Oldmire then stepped into the hallway, appraising the maintenance chief pointedly.

"I spoke with Ms. Willard-Stew... Willard... I spoke with Joan earlier in the week, and she told me to stop by," Brian shrugged and blushed at his inability to properly pronounce the hyphenated name. "But I can come back after she returns."

"No, no, it's probably better that you get your work done while she's out. Here, let me open the door for you." Ms. Oldmire exited her room at last and withdrew her set of keys before unlocking the door for him and stepping aside.

"Thank you. You wouldn't have any idea what the issue was would you?" Brian smiled questioningly at her as he stepped into the small apartment and began to open his bag to find a flashlight.

"I think Charlie's..." Ms. Oldmire began before stopping abruptly. Brian could only imagine what was going through her mind. Were he in her place... frankly he wouldn't have any idea what to do. For the moment, he was thankful for something mundane to put his hands to.

"I know about the girl, I'm... I'm very sorry, and I have all of my team looking for her," Brian mentioned gently. "I can start in her room though, if that seems to be a trouble spot."

Ms. Oldmire nodded in silence as the taller man walked to the closed door of Charlie's bedroom and opened it softly.

Brian had barely set foot into the room when his breath caught. He heard the distant crash of a tool bag hitting the floor and a sudden pain in his left foot, but ignored it all completely, for there, bundled sweetly in the covers of the bed lay a pretty young girl.

"Charlie?" Ms. Oldmire's voice was tense as she leapt to the door with surprising quickness, having responded instantly to the maintenance chief's shock. "Charlie!... Charlie! Oh, my dear, Charlie... Charlie is that you... is that really you?"

Brian stood dumbly in the frame of the small bedroom door as the older woman nearly shouldered him to the ground in her rush to get past him to the girl. In a blink, she was kneeling at the edge of the bed, nearly in tears as the young girl lazily blinked and yawned... opening her eyes and smiling.

"Auntie Goldie? Isn't Aunt Nonie home yet? I've had the strangest dream..."

Chapter 54

The next several hours had flown by in a blur. Ms. Oldmire, or Auntie Goldie as Charlie called her, had whisked the girl up into an embrace, pinching her cheeks until she yelped, and then hurriedly helped her dress before pulling her into the kitchen for a meal. The older woman wouldn't let her eyes off the girl for even a moment as she dashed about the kitchen, pulling pots and pans about and making a racket as she alternated between tears and chuckles.

To Brian's eye her every movement shouted, *What news! What glorious news!*

When the shock had worn away enough for Goldie to notice the dumbfounded presence of Brian standing about and staring at the pair of them, she shooed him out of the apartment with strict orders to track down Joan immediately, which is how Brian found himself moving from floor to floor while radioing his small team to find Joan and let her know that her daughter had returned.

A crackling reply from his radio alerted him that Ms. Willard-Stewart had last been seen outside sitting on one of the benches in the cold air, which sent Brian racing like a madman back through the halls, down the elevator, and out the front door, uncaring as to who would see him.

And there she was.

Shivering, and huddled in her winter coat, Joan sat alone with eyes cast to the concrete at her feet as snow fell around her in large wet flakes.

"Joan..." Brian called as he ran up to her, out of breath. "Joan..."

But the woman's eyes remained frozen to the pavement until he gently took her shoulder. And as her eyes turned to his, he could see the shell of a woman. She had clearly been crying and likely hadn't slept in the days that had passed since Charlie's disappearance.

"Charlie's back..." Brian said with urgency, just now catching his breath from the all-out sprint.

"That isn't funny, Brian..." Joan shook her head and shrugged her shoulder away from him.

Kneeling beside her, Brian tried again, "It's the truth, Joan. I don't know how, but I saw her with my own eyes. Ms. Oldmire, your neighbor, is with her now... come on... it's all over, let's get you home."

This time, fresh tears were glistening in Joan's eyes as they met Brian's, and, within, he could see a small sliver of hope.

Then, she was on her feet, unsteady at first, but gaining strength with every step as Brian helped her back into the building, through the lobby, up the express elevator, and back to her room.

"Charlie! Oh Charlie... Charlie... don't you ever... ever do that to me again... I'm just... oh, Charlie."

As the pair embraced, Brian felt oddly out of place and let himself slide out the door, closing it softly behind him as he turned back to the bank of elevators. "Well... maybe she isn't so unlucky after all."

Chapter 55

A knock came at the door as Joan and Charlie sat together at the kitchen table, sharing a light lunch as they continued to process all that had happened. Charlie had not felt comfortable talking about where she had been and wasn't entirely certain if her strange adventure was anything more than an elaborate dream. Instead, she had concocted a flimsy story about being lost and a kind resident who had taken care of her.

Joan didn't believe any of it, and for a time had persisted in trying to find out where and why Charlie had run off. But she had given up for now, only too happy that her daughter was home and safe again.

Unexpectedly, a knock at the door interrupted their cozy silence. Joan stood from the table and made her way across the small living room to the door, opening it slowly to discover an unwelcome sight that shocked her back to reality.

"Hello, Ms. Willard-Stewart. May I come in?"

Standing before her just outside the door was the primly appointed figure of Ms. Filmore, the Child Services officer. With a lump growing in her gut, Joan pulled the door wide and waved the woman in. "Please, come in."

Ms. Filmore's eyes caught on Charlie at the table, who looked back at her quizzically. "I had heard that Charlie had returned. I'm very glad for you," the woman offered as she stepped inside, holding her briefcase and waiting for Joan to suggest a place for them to sit.

"Charlie... please go to your room." Joan's request was quietly spoken but contradicted by Ms. Filmore's response.

"Actually, I was hoping that I could speak to both of you, if that's alright."

"Oh... I suppose. How about you just join us at the table here then," Joan suggested, adding, "Would you like some lunch? We've made some fresh hummus and there's plenty."

"Thank you, but that won't be necessary." Ms. Filmore's voice was curt and formal, but not impolite. Taking a seat in a third chair, Ms. Filmore clicked her briefcase open and withdrew a thick file of papers. "You've made quite a bit of work for me, Miss Charlotte," the officer remarked while setting the papers on the table and folding her hands across the top. "I can't say that I know what to make of all of this. I hope that you have learned your lesson young woman, and that you won't be scaring your aunt... your mother, like that again." Ms. Filmore corrected herself, as she recalled her prior conversation with Joan.

Young Charlie looked first to her Aunt Nonie, who nodded gently, before replying. "I have definitely learned my lesson, ma'am. I love my Aunt Nonie and wouldn't want to be anywhere else in the world." She smiled brightly as she caught sight of Joan biting her lip and looking away.

"Well, I had hoped you might be open to an opportunity that presented itself recently." Ms. Filmore lifted her hands from the folder and opened it to reveal a brochure inside, featuring images of a beautiful apartment building. "I'm not one for beating around the bush. It appears that your story has found its way to some very generous people. These people happen to have a beautiful apartment open that they would like to make available to you for a... reasonable price."

Of all the things she had expected to hear the next time this woman came to visit her, this had never crossed Joan's mind. So shocked was she that she merely sat still, stunned into silence as she watched Charlie reach for the colorful brochure and open the pages excitedly to exclaim over this or that detail.

Having noted Joan's reaction, Ms. Filmore turned her gaze to the woman and added in softer tones, "I, and apparently a few others, believe that it's time you had something go right for a change. This... This offer is legitimate. And before you think about refusing, I must warn you that I cannot condone you remaining in this apartment in its current state with this little girl."

Joan choked back a sob as tears welled in her eyes. "But... but I ..."

"There's a playground!" exclaimed Charlie excitedly.

"Actually, I believe it is much better than that," corrected Ms. Filmore. "This particular apartment building is just a block away from the school where your sister attends. There's still paperwork to be done, but I've reviewed the public schools in the area, and I believe that we can get Charlie enrolled for the next trimester."

Joan found it difficult to respond as tears streamed freely down her cheeks. All she could do was watch as Charlie squealed with delight and leapt up from her chair to gather Ms. Filmore into a tight embrace.

Chapter 56

Days had passed since Charlie's return, and life had almost returned to normal for the small family in apartment forty-three twelve. A crew of workers had been in and out of their house, helping to pack up their few belongings for the move to the new building across town. And now, only a few days before Christmas, Charlie sat on the small, cushioned bench in the building's lobby, looking up at the tall and beautifully decorated Christmas tree. She had never seen a Christmas tree here before, in fact, she had never seen any decorations in the building.

Today was the day that her sister was coming home, and no amount of scolding or threatening could convince Charlie to wait back in the apartment. Not wanting to argue any longer, her Aunt Nonie had acquiesced and allowed Charlie to wait in the lobby, which she was doing when she noticed a pretty little package resting neatly under the tree.

Looking around and seeing that none of the few residents passing through were paying attention to her, Charlie hopped off the stool and approached the medium sized box with growing curiosity.

It was beautifully wrapped in bright red shiny paper with a silvery bow and covered with sparkling snowflake designs.

"Well... what an odd little thing to find just one present sitting here," Charlie noted as she drew closer to the box and nestled herself down onto her knees to get a closer look. "And I see that you have a tag. Well, perhaps someone just forgot their present. Let's see where you belong, shall we?" she commented as her hand took hold of the small tag and turned it over.

"To the little girl they call Charlie," Charlie read with great surprise. "Do you think that's for me?"

"I do think so, actually," replied a voice from behind her.

"Oh!" exclaimed Charlie as she stood quickly and dusted glitter from the skirt she had picked for her sister's return.

"Oh. My apologies," replied the older man with a kind smile. "I seem to surprise quite a few people these days. But I do believe that the gift is yours if your name is indeed Charlie. Go ahead... open it up." The elderly man smiled again as he stood watching with a twinkle in his eye and a knowing smile.

"My Aunt Nonie would not like me talking to strangers," replied Charlie, though she had already stooped to pick up the gift and was picking away at the folded wrapping-paper along one edge.

"And your Aunt Nonie is a wise woman. Though I think this one small gift will be safe enough. But if it makes you feel any better, I'll be on my way. It's a very busy time after all." The older man smiled again and offered a little bow before turning and striding toward the revolving doors and out into the night.

Unable to contain her excitement, Charlie tore the remaining paper away, opened the box, and gasped at the sight of a beautiful pair of red boots that lay nestled inside.

"Where on earth did you get those?" The voice of her Aunt Nonie surprised Charlie into dropping the box to the ground and hiding her hands in her pockets guiltily.

"He told me to open them, I... I wasn't stealing anything," replied Charlie defensively.

"But that's... It's... not possible," responded her Aunt Nonie without any condemnation in her voice at all. Curious, Joan approached the box and lifted it from the ground, seeing the exact pair of boots she had marveled at in the department store weeks ago. Folded neatly inside was a small note that she lifted out as she handed the box back to Charlie.

"Dear Joan, I hope you won't think poorly of me if I offer this small gift of cheer to you and your dear Charlie. Perhaps our paths will cross again someday. Until then, may you have the very merriest Christmas." The note was signed simply, R. Kerstman.

Charlie was already trying the boots on and exclaimed, "They fit perfectly! Can I keep them? Please can I keep them?"

Joan blinked back a rush of emotion as she smiled and nodded, and as she lifted her eyes, she could see the school van pull up outside and the familiar figure of Cassie stepping out with bags in tow. "Cassie is here..." Joan said, but Charlie and her boots were already running full tilt to the doors and out into the light snowfall, the little golden bells jingling softly with each step.

Chapter 57

The sisters caught each other in a tight embrace, laughing as tears flowed and as they twirled each other about while soft snowflakes filtered down from the dark night sky, glistening as the lights from the walkway illuminated them.

"Oh, I've missed you so much!" Charlie cried as she hugged her sister closely. "You'll never guess what happened to me! And oh, do you know that we're moving! We'll be right next to you, and I can see you every day! And... you just wouldn't believe all the strange things that have gone on, but I can't tell anyone but you because no one will believe me!"

Charlie went on and on as her sister laughed and hugged her. Soon, they were both swept into a big hug by Aunt Nonie who could wait inside no longer. And then Joan was ushering them back toward the warmth, murmuring something about being worried about them catching a cold.

It was then, as Charlie held tightly to her sister's waist, and before they had gone inside, that her eye caught something moving at the edge of the light near a bush along the walkway. Breaking free of her sister's warm embrace, Charlie kept her eyes pinned to the section of the bushes where she had seen the movement—running quickly to the edge of the walkway and getting down on her knees. It took a moment for Charlie's eyes to adjust to the shadows as she peered intently in and around the base of the small boxwood.

"Is that you... Is it really you?" Charlie asked in a whisper.

She saw another flitting motion caught between the light and shadow as her sister and aunt worriedly came to her side and pulled her back to her feet, dusting snow from her and murmuring worriedly at her.

Their words slid from Charlie's ears like a familiar ambient sound, for in a moment between breaths, Charlie thought she heard a small, familiar voice chitter in response...

"Very bright... Veeeerrrry bright."

~THE END~

Acknowledgements

First and always, thank you to my lovely wife Rachael who has weathered the ups and downs, ins and outs, and all the in-betweens. I love you and cannot imagine a world without you.

Thank you to my children Katherine, Hannah, Joshua, and Mason for helping to bring this whole story adventure to life. Thank you Dad for the generous spirit that inspired Mr. Kerstman. And thank you Mom for being my first beta reader, biggest fan, and for instilling in me a love for creating long ago.

A special thank you to Marni MacRae, who provided the detailed edit that my manuscript so desperately needed, and to Sheryl Soong for the amazing cover and illustrations that help to bring the story to life.

I also owe a deep debt of gratitude to the many voice actors and friends in podcasting I have made along the way to list just a few: Mike Atchley, Brad Zimmerman, Josh Monroe, Jonah Jackson, Alixandria Young-Jui, Kenneth Eckle, Nikki and Jordache Richardson, Corey Pfautsch, Carrie Coello, Jessica Ann, Ditrie Marie Bowie, Susannah Lewis the whole crew at PodiconGo, Dice Tower Theatre, the Cast Junkie Discord community, and to Joleen Fresquez who voiced Charlie so beautifully in the original audio version of this story on the HappyGoLukky podcast.

About the Author

Daniel holds a Bachelor of Arts degree from Grove City College, Pennsylvania, a Master of Arts in Counseling and Master of Divinity from Asbury Theological Seminary, and a Master of Business Administration from the University of Maryland's Robert H. Smith School of Business.

Daniel's story as a Navy Chaplain was featured in a book by author Jane Hampton Cook in 2006, and several of his letters written during his combat experience supporting Operation Iraqi Freedom in 2003 were published in the book titled: *Stories of Faith and Courage from the War in Iraq and Afghanistan.*

Daniel, along with his son Mason, launched HappyGoLukky Productions in 2019, resulting in the creation of the HappyGoLukky family friendly storytelling podcast that reached a peak rank of #21 on Apple Podcasts. Their storytelling improv sessions contributed directly to the creation of *Charlie Saves Christmas*, the prologue novella to the *Chronicles of Eridul* series.

Daniel resides in Pittsburgh, Pennsylvania with his wife Rachael and their puppy Penny. Their four children have begun to fly the nest, as children should.